THE NEW NEIGHBOR

A CORIO HEIGHTS NOVEL

RYE COX

Cover Art: Qlu

Editing: Royal Editing Services

Proofreading: M.A. Hinkle, Charity VanHuss

For my family, blood or found. This story wouldn't exist without your encouragement.

ONE

CALEB

"Mother finger nuggets!" I shouted as I hit my head for the millionth time on the corner cabinet in my kitchen. You'd think I would be used to the too-low-hanging cabinet I had the misfortune of having in my tiny kitchen after living in the same apartment for over two years, but nope. I hit the damn thing. Every. Single. Time.

I turned my head toward the loud thump that had startled me into hitting my head in the first place. It had come from the apartment next door to mine—the apartment that should have been empty, but obviously wasn't.

My last neighbor in the unit beside mine had left three months ago, taking with them the drum set they used to bang on in the middle of the damn night. I was pretty sure everyone in the building had filed a complaint to the building manager to have him evicted. Good riddance.

I don't think I'm a hard guy to get along with, but when you keep me up all night with that *thump thump thump*, not even baking can bring me back to my happy place. The rhythmic thumping rippled through my body and brought up unpleasant memories to the surface.

Baking had always been the one thing that centered me when I was stressed or having a hard time. When I was younger, I loved Sunday mornings with my dad where we were always baking one thing or another. On our last Sunday together, our laughter rang out as Mom barged into our little sanctuary carrying my fussy one-year-old brother. Dad was the only one who could calm Conner down when he was in one of his moods. As Dad placated the baby, Mom tried to sneak a piece of the unfinished dessert. Dad pretended to get mad at her, but he'd let her "steal" an extra piece anyway.

Baking Sundays were my favorite day of the week. We'd laugh, talk about silly things, and enjoy the sweet smells in the kitchen until we got to dig in and enjoy our handiwork. It was perfect...Until it wasn't.

I was lying in bed on the worst Saturday night of my life leafing through a book of baking recipes, trying to find one for the next day. I found the perfect recipe to try out—Triple Chocolate Layer Cake, because what eleven-year-old boy wasn't addicted to chocolate? I saved the page to show my dad later and closed my eyes, excited for the morning to come so that we could create chocolate magic that would probably have had me jumping off the walls all day.

Morning had come earlier than normal.

It was the loud *thump thump thump* that woke me up. The Cookie Monster clock I had gotten for my ninth birthday sat on my nightstand, proclaiming it to be two a.m.

"Mommy?" I called out toward the sliver of light peeking through my cracked door.

"Go back to sleep, honey. Your dad probably just got home." Her slippers shuffled past my door and down the stairs. I jumped out of bed and rushed downstairs to see my dad. He had left three days ago on a business trip, but he had promised to come back in time for Baking Sunday. Dad always kept his promises.

"I don't know why he didn't use his keys." Mom's voice was thick with sleep, and I ran to catch up with her. The *thump thump thump* got louder the closer we got to the front door.

"One moment!" Mom called out. She flipped the switch for the front door light and looked out the peephole. She frowned at whatever she saw out there. "Get behind me," she said to me.

I was good at following instructions. Dad always let me measure out the ingredients while he read out the recipe to me. "What's better than learning while having fun?" he would say as he sneakily hid away the tablespoon. He taught me conversions at a young age. One tablespoon was equal to three teaspoons. One cup was equal to four quarter cups. One week was equal to seven days until we could bake again.

Mom opened the door a crack. I peeked out from behind her and saw two police officers wet from the rain.

"Can I help you?" Mom asked.

"Are you Maryann Turner? Wife of Dillan Turner?" the one with the beard asked. He looked at her with kind, sympathetic eyes. Eyes that said *I'm about to deliver some bad news.*

Thunder rang out from behind him. Lightning streaked our faces a ghastly white.

Okay, maybe there was no thunder or lightning since there had only been a light drizzle. Maybe that was something my child brain conjured up since in movies, bad news was *always* delivered in terrible weather. Thunder accompanied news like a strike to the heart. Well, what the police delivered was bad news. The worst news. My dad wasn't going to keep his promise.

It was a car accident, they said. A truck lost control due to the slippery road and hit my dad's car head on. He died on impact.

I couldn't comprehend what they meant when they said my dad was *gone*. My dad was gone every few months because of his job, but he was always *back*. I knew how to count days because my dad taught me when I was younger. Every time I closed my eyes for the night, a new day would come. That meant that if I closed my eyes three nights in a row, I would be able to see my dad again.

And so, that was what I did. I closed my eyes and prayed for the nightmare to end. I wanted the real morning to come, not this false, still too dark—why would anyone be awake at this time—two a.m. I wanted to see my dad's smiling face waiting for me in the kitchen.

I held my hands over my ears, hoping to drown out my mom's words of *gone* and *forever* because she didn't know what she was talking about. Dad *always* kept his promises. He said three days.

Ringing was the last thing I heard that night. My mom's words droned away in the background along with the police officers' concerned voices. Everything seemed fake. It was like a nightmare that felt endless, but probably only took as long as the time it took for your alarm clock to ring. And ring. And ring. Until the nightmare ended and you were brought back to reality.

This time, the ringing didn't end that nightmare, nor did the ringing stop.

I looked up from my daze, where I had been staring at the wall that separated me from the nonexistent thumping that had once come from my annoying neighbor's drum set at the ungodly hour of two a.m. The ringing I had heard in my memories didn't end when I came back to the present. I was startled to find that the timer on my phone was notifying me to check on my cookies.

Turning off the timer, I turned back to my oven to make sure that my daze hadn't lasted longer than I'd thought. I hoped the cookies weren't burnt—they weren't, thank God.

I let them cool on the counter for a few minutes before trying one. Satisfied with how it tasted, I loaded them on a plate to give this batch as a welcoming gift.

It was time to meet the new neighbor.

TWO

ZACK

I turned back to the mess of spilled clothes and accessories made from the pile of toppled-over boxes lying on the floor of my new bedroom.

"Dude, I told you not to put the heavy box on top of all the other ones," my best friend Eric called out from the kitchen. He'd volunteered to help me move and was currently in the process of unpacking my plates and bowls and putting them in random cabinets.

"My bad. I hope that didn't disturb my neighbors." It didn't look like this apartment had thin walls, but I wouldn't be surprised if that crash had been heard from across the street.

Eric looked back at me, waggling his eyebrows. "You better hope that the walls aren't thin here. You'll be keeping your neighbors up with all your hookups."

"You're one to talk. Who was it again that overslept today because they had a sex marathon last night? I mean seriously, it's long past our college days. Are you part bunny or some-thing?" I liked sex as much as the next guy, but I was usually a one and done for the night. I had never had much interest in going multiple rounds in a night, at least not with the same guy.

"Oh, right. I forgot who I was talking to. I guess they didn't cure you when you got it checked out in college. Tough, bro. It's been years," he snickered.

I threw a sock at him. I hoped it came from the pile of dirty laundry I hadn't had the chance to wash before shoving into a random box. That was what he deserved for bringing up the dark days before I had figured out my sexuality and had thought I had an actual problem with my dick.

"Not funny, man! You know how worried I was about having erectile dysfunction. And you know that my nuts—"

A knock came from the door. The *open* door I forgot to close from our last run down to the car. A cute man stood at the doorway holding a plate of cookies. A deep blush crept up his neck. His eyes flitted around under his glasses as if he was looking for an escape route.

"Hi," he squeaked. "I'm your next-door neighbor. I brought you white chocolate macadamia nut cookies." His eyes widened when he realized what he said.

"I mean I brought you cookies. But they do have macadamia nuts in them, so I should probably tell you in case you have a nut allergy, and oh my God, I need to stop saying nut." His eyes were still shifting around, looking *anywhere* but at me. "Sorry, I think I came at a bad time. I'll come back later."

"Wait a second," I called as he turned to leave. This was just my luck. I got a cute guy for a neighbor, and now he thought I had ED *and* a problem with my balls. I couldn't let him leave like this.

I hurried to the door in case he actually made a run for it. "My name's Zack. Nice to meet you." I offered my hand up for a handshake. He stared at it like it was going to bite him. An awkward beat passed before he worked up the courage to accept it. I didn't let go of his hand.

"I'm Eric, this idiot's best friend," Eric called from the kitchen, not to be left out.

"Hey! I'm not an idiot, you dickhead!" Eric rolled his eyes and continued unpacking the box he was currently working on.

"Caleb," my new neighbor said, the corners of his mouth tilted slightly upwards in amusement.

"Sorry you had to hear that. We were just joking around. I don't actually have ED." I had to make sure he knew that. There was nothing more important in the world right now than making sure my new, *cute* neighbor understood that I *did not* have ED.

"What?" he asked, looking genuinely confused.

"You know, erectile dysfunction. Also, there's nothing wrong with my balls either. I have perfectly normal balls." Okay, maybe I shouldn't have said that. Eric laughing hysterically in the background like the jerk he was made it even more apparent that I'd put my foot in my mouth in front of the new neighbor yet again. "Sorry, I'm not normally this weird. I promise."

"Yes, he is."

I shot Eric a death glare. I didn't know why I considered that traitor my best friend. He obviously thrived on my misery.

"Um..." Caleb glanced down at the handshake I refused to release him from.

"Oh, my bad." I reluctantly let go of his warm hand. They weren't soft like I imagined a clean-cut guy like him to have. No, they were callused from burns that were common in hands that toiled in the kitchen.

He shifted his feet and thrust the plate between us.

"Here," he said. "A 'welcome to the building' gift."

"Thanks, I love sweets." I accepted the plate and grabbed a cookie.

He shot forward and placed a hand on mine to stop me. "I wasn't kidding about the macadamia nuts. You don't have a nut allergy or anything, do you?"

"No, I don't. I don't have a problem with *any* kind of nuts."

His eyes widened at my innuendo, and the pink that was finally starting to disappear from his cheeks crept up again. I winked at him. I couldn't help it. He looked so cute when he blushed.

I took a bite of the sweet-smelling cookie and groaned.

"Oh my god, these are orgasms in my mouth. You baked these? Are you a baker?" I threw the rest of the cookie in my mouth and reached for another one. I could probably gobble down this whole plate today.

He nodded shyly. "I'm glad you like them. And I do bake, but I'm not a professional baker. It's just for fun."

"Well, these are amazing. If you had a bakery, I'd visit every day," I said, no lie in my words. The cookies were worth killing for.

"Gimme, gimme. I want some too." Eric stalked his way toward me, eyes focused solely on the plate. He made a grab for a cookie. I swerved out of his reach. While we were both pretty bulky guys, Eric was half a head taller than me, but I was faster.

"Nuh-uh, you heard Caleb. These are to welcome me to the building. You're not getting any." I wasn't going to share the gift my terribly shy but adorable new neighbor had gotten me, especially after Eric had made it his personal mission to embarrass me in front of Caleb.

"Don't be like that. Come on! Just one!" He lunged for the plate again.

I dodged out of the way, using my other hand to protect the cookies. "Hey! You're gonna make me spill them."

Caleb stood there chuckling behind his hand. He looked younger when he smiled. He wasn't old—probably younger than my twenty-eight years—but you could see the stress of life in his eyes. They seemed to carry the weight of something no twenty-year-old should be carrying. But when he smiled, his whole face lifted, and his burdens disappeared, leaving behind a charming youthfulness that I could get addicted to staring at.

"Well, I better let you finish settling in. Welcome to the building." He walked back to the entrance and paused. "I'll, uh, close the door for you as well."

"Thanks again for these." I lifted the plate. "I'll return the plate to you later."

He waved his hand, and with a click of the door, he was gone.

"Someone's got a little crush," Eric singsonged behind me.

"Shh!" I ran toward the door to make sure it was completely closed and locked it for good measure. "I do not have a crush. I just think he's cute, is all." I walked back to the kitchen and placed the plate on the counter, taking another cookie so that I could savor it this time.

"You were rambling. You never ramble. You were always as cool as a cucumber for school presentations." He snatched a cookie, and I couldn't even be bothered to bitch at him this time.

"That's because you were doing all you could to embarrass me in front of him. It didn't help that he is totally my type." I finished off my cookie and moved the plate away from him. "These are mine. No more for you."

I made my way back into my bedroom to assess the damage from the avalanche of boxes that had fallen earlier. It was going to take a while to get everything sorted, and there was no need for both of us to suffer late into the night.

"Hey, you can take off. I'll do the rest. Thanks for your help, man," I called back out to the kitchen.

"Sounds good. I'll get out of your hair." Eric's voice sounded rushed, and frantic rummaging came from outside the room. *What the heck was he doing out there?*

I turned to leave the room to check out what was going on.

"Make sure to give Lady hugs and kisses for—"

The sound of the door banging shut cut off my sentence. He was gone before I even returned to the kitchen. The once-full plate of cookies was now half empty. That bastard.

THREE

CALEB

My new neighbor was hot. And probably, most likely, gay. Oh my god. I had a new, hot, and *gay* neighbor.

Zack wasn't what I had expected. He looked like the typical jock, but he didn't act like one. He joked around with his friend like they were kids in front of a virtual stranger and had no qualms in doing so. And he acted a bit shy, or at least embarrassed, in front of me. *Me*, the least intimidating person in the world. Sure, I was an inch or so taller than him, but I was half his size in terms of muscle. He could probably snap me like a twig if he wanted to, not that he would have any reason to do that. I hoped.

I thought back to how his large hands had enveloped mine. They weren't soft, but they weren't as callused as mine either. They felt...just right. I had wanted to hold his hand longer, but I could feel my hands breaking out in nervous sweat, and I hadn't wanted him to notice.

It was hard to get anything done after meeting Zack. My thoughts kept returning to him. I wondered if he was single, and if he was, could he be interested in me? It felt like he was flirting with me, but I always had a hard time telling. My friends ribbed me for being the densest person in the world. They said I wouldn't know I was being flirted with even if the other person explicitly told me they were flirting with me. I agreed with them. Flirting was hard. Why did humans need to flirt? Why couldn't we court like some species of animals did? They could, I don't know, give me a pebble or something and make it super clear they were interested.

The best part about living in the same building as my best friend was that I could pop downstairs to his apartment and ask the random questions my brain would obsess over, except Ian worked on Saturdays and he wouldn't get off for a few more hours, and I would go crazy if I kept thinking about this until then.

I finally managed to sort out my thoughts and get some work done. I had enough ingredients to make another batch of white chocolate macadamia nut cookies for tomorrow. I had a weekly scheduled brunch with my mom and little brother on Sundays. With Mom working six days a week at the diner and Conner participating in afterschool programs, it was, unfortunately, the only time we got to see each other.

I worried that Mom never had any time to date. I didn't want her to be alone forever. This year would be the fifteenth year since my dad's passing, but I had never seen Mom go on a single date in all those years. She said she was happy with just her two boys, but I suspected she was still lonely. While Conner turned seventeen next month, being the little genius that he was, he had skipped a grade in elementary school. That meant he would head off to college soon, leaving Mom all alone in the house. It was a worry I constantly brought up to Mom when I nagged her to find someone new. She called me silly every time I brought it up.

It was late by the time I finished the cookies. Once they

cooled, I placed them into a container and set them on the counter to take with me tomorrow. As I lay in bed, thoughts of my new green-eyed neighbor flowed through my head until I drifted off to sleep.

I woke up early the next morning, the sunrise barely peeking over the horizon. It was perfect weather for my morning run. I was fortunate enough to live a ten-minute walk from the beach since Ian knew the owner of our building and got us in at a steal.

I always had my morning runs at the beach. The clean breeze cleared my head and had the ability to blow any troubles I had away. And I needed that today.

I couldn't stop thinking of my interaction with my new neighbor yesterday, and I even dreamed about it in my sleep. Dreams of me awkwardly stuttering while Zack and his friend laughed at the embarrassment that I was. I wasn't a kid anymore, for crying out loud. Even if I did have a crush on my new neighbor, not saying that I did (okay, maybe just a teeny-tiny crush), I shouldn't be having dreams about people laughing at me for who I was or how I acted.

I was a grown-ass man who was responsible for his family. Not the little kid who was made fun of as a child because his dad wasn't there. It wasn't his fault he wasn't there. He was dead. But kids didn't understand that. They only saw that I was missing a dad, and my mom was working all the time to support my brother and me.

The sun was fully out thirty minutes into my run. The ocean breeze kept me cool and refreshed, and it was the perfect March morning in Corio City. The winter cold had gone back into hibernation, but it wasn't blisteringly hot yet.

A few miles down the beach stood a lighthouse. I always paused my runs there, sitting on my usual bench that faced the ocean to take a break.

When I was younger, my dad would take me to the lighthouse in the city we used to live in and tell me stories of sailors getting lost at sea. He said ships often got lost during storms in the past. That was why lighthouses were built. As a beacon of hope and a guide to show them the way home and away from potential dangers.

I used to wonder if things would've been different if we had a lighthouse that night. Maybe Dad had gotten lost in the storm, and that was why he couldn't find his way home. The lighthouse could have guided him away from the truck that had taken his life. Of course, I hadn't considered that he wasn't a sailor, or at sea, but that didn't stop my childish thoughts.

After resting for a bit, I jogged my way back home. I had enough time to shower, head to the grocery store, and make it to Mom's before brunch. The unpleasant dream from the night before finally disappeared from the front of my thoughts.

Mom lived a thirty-minute drive from my apartment. She was usually too busy during the week to shop, so I would stop by the store on my way to her house and pick up their weekly groceries.

It wasn't long before I pulled into the driveway of a cozy blue bungalow. We had moved back to Corio City, Mom's hometown, after Dad's death. With two kids in tow and no family to support her, Mom struggled to raise us. We lived in an old, two-bedroom apartment that barely fit the needs of two growing boys. But we made it work, and Mom had worked hard to purchase this house when I was in college. It wasn't anything fancy, but it was hers. Well, it would be hers once she finished paying off her thirty-five-year mortgage.

I helped her with the mortgage when she let me, but she rarely did. So, I did other things to help her instead. Like buying the groceries or whatever materials Conner needed for his robots. I wished I was able to pay off the whole thing outright for her so that she didn't have to worry about money.

Another reason why you should get your CPA. The voice in the back of my head was very loud this time. It was something I had been considering for a while now.

Working as an accountant made decent money, but it didn't afford me much left over to completely support my mom and brother. If I got my CPA, I would be able to make more, but I didn't know if that was what I truly wanted. I disliked my job on a normal day and despised it during tax season, which we were currently in the middle of. I didn't want to invest so much money to get the license if I wasn't going to use it in the future.

I juggled grocery bags onto one hand and used my key to unlock the front door with the other.

"Mom, I'm here," I called out. She bustled about in the kitchen preparing our brunch while Conner sat on the couch watching a documentary. "Hey, kid. I have more bags in the car. Help me bring them in."

He paused the documentary and ran out of the house. He was a good egg. Most teens his age were in their rebellious phase. Not him, though. He helped out when he could.

I dropped the bags on the kitchen counter, then turned to give my mom a kiss on her cheek. She looked more tired than usual, the bags under her eyes a glaring indication that she wasn't getting enough rest.

"How was your week, honey?" Even when she was exhausted, she still had to make sure that I was all right.

"Tax season has been killer, but it's almost over." I grabbed a piece of the cold macaroni she had made for brunch. She swatted at my hand for stealing the food before it was ready. "I also got a new neighbor," I said, a bit more shyly than I would have liked.

She glanced up from her chopping, eyebrow raised.

"A boy?" she asked. She was always able to read my mind. I used to think she was psychic.

I leaned against the counter, feigning nonchalance. "Yeah, he moved in yesterday."

"And?"

"And I gave him cookies to welcome him to the building." I glanced at my fingernails like they were the most interesting things in the world.

"And?" She always knew when there was something more.

"And I think he was flirting with me, but I'm not sure because I haven't had the chance to evaluate the whole interaction with Ian yet," I confessed, the words tumbling out of my mouth. I never kept anything from her for long.

"You should ask him out on a date. It's time for you to settle down. I was already married and had you by the time I was your age."

I rolled my eyes. She said the same thing every time. "I have plenty of time to find love. You guys need me more."

"Caleb, we—" Conner bounded in with the rest of the bags before she could finish her sentence. Mom's brows furrowed as she gave me a look that said this wasn't over. She had told me numerous times that she felt guilty about the pressure I put on myself to support her and Conner, but I couldn't help it. Just as I was all they had, they were also all I had.

I nudged Conner's shoulder with my own as I joined him on the couch to finish watching the movie. Coincidently, he was watching a documentary about animal mating habits in the wild. Certain spiders and birds danced to attract their mates.

Male elephants fanned their ears to spread their scents to find a mate. And penguins gave their mate a pebble. I knew I'd had something there. Humans should also give pebbles instead of, ugh, flirting.

Brunch was filled with laughter and the comforting feelings of home. Conner told us about his week at school and the latest robot he was creating. Mom told stories of the interesting customers that had visited the diner this week—there was never a lack of those stories—and I almost fell off my seat numerous times from laughter.

Conner had plans with his friends to tinker with their robots that afternoon. He helped clean up, and, with a hug and kiss for both my mom and me, he was gone.

Mom fidgeted with the dish towel, her eyebrows furrowed with stress and worry.

"What's up?" I grabbed the dish towel from her and took over drying the dishes.

She bit her lower lip and paused. There was only one thing my mom ever hesitated talking about. Money. She disliked the idea of ever receiving help and hated it even more coming from her son. When I was getting my degree in a career that didn't interest me, she had apologized to me for being a failure as a mother because she wasn't able to give me the chance to pursue my dreams. She didn't want me to choose a stable job over my passion, but I was adamant. I would do anything for them because she and Conner were the best people on Earth. And no matter how many times I told her how thankful I was to have her as a mother, she couldn't understand her worth.

"Did something happen?" I broke the silence.

"It's nothing bad. It's just...Conner wants to participate in some kind of robotics competition this summer. You know my car broke down the other week, and I had to spend a fortune to get it fixed. Money has been a little tight since then." Her shoulders slumped, and more worry lines marred her face. She hated needing my help financially.

"I always said that piece of junk took more maintenance than a diva," I joked to lighten the mood. "How much does he need?"

Her eyes glinted at my sassy statement. "Three thousand. He'll need that much for the sign-up fee as well as money to buy the parts he's eyeing for his robot." She paused, her fingers picking at her hangnail. It was a bad habit she had when she was nervous. "I have about half of that saved. Conner said there are cash prizes for winning the competition too, so we can return the money if he..."

"Mom, stop." I cut her off. "You know I'm more than happy to help out. That's what family is for."

Tears pooled at the corner of her eyes when she looked up at me. I reached out to envelop her in a bear hug. She used to hug me like that when I was a kid, and I wondered when I'd gotten so big that I had begun holding her in my arms instead of the other way around.

It was sad to say, but the money Conner needed would deplete most of my savings. It was time to seriously consider my future. I meant it when I said I would do anything for my family, and that included getting my CPA and working in a field I hated.

FOUR

ZACK

Monday mornings were always a drag. I hadn't gotten over my exhaustion from unpacking all weekend. Moving sucked, but it helped that I got a cute new neighbor, especially one that knew how to bake.

I found reasons to leave my apartment numerous times on Sunday, but I didn't catch a single glimpse of him. However, that didn't stop me from glancing at his door Monday morning as I left for work. His door was firmly shut, just like the last ten or so times I passed by it yesterday.

I wheeled my bike down the hall and waited for the elevator to arrive. One of the main reasons I'd moved to this apartment building was because it was only a ten-minute bike ride from my office. Since I was a restaurant consultant who had numerous clients outside the city, I had my car for when I needed to take business trips, but most of the time, I preferred to leisurely bike around the city.

I had a week-long business trip outside of Corio City last week, and then I had to pack and move everything as soon as I came back. After all the stress that had accumulated from the long week and weekend, a refreshing ride on my bike would do me some good.

It was nine o'clock by the time I got to the office. I usually arrived early, but I guess the past week had exhausted me more than I thought. Traveling was the part of the job that I used to love, but the thrill I used to get from it had greatly diminished. When you had traveled to as many cities as I had, they all blended together. Or maybe I was just getting older.

Scott was already sitting in the cubicle next to mine when I arrived to my floor. His head shot up as soon as he caught sight of me, and he waved me over.

"Dude, you picked the worst day to be late," Scott whispered, his eyes shifting around the office.

"Why are you so nervous?" I gave him a light push. He was acting weirder than normal.

"Dude, I think our new manager has it out for you. He was grumbling about your absence Friday."

My eyebrow furrowed in confusion. "What? New manager? What happened to Nick?"

"Dunno, man. Heard he was suddenly transferred to another branch. Apparently, our new manager has more experience, so they wanted him at headquarters. He transferred over while you were away on your business trip. Anyway, just keep your head down today. I think he's gonna call you into his office later."

He glanced around one more time before pushing me out of his cubicle and fixing his gaze intently on his computer screen.

Weird. It was like everything had changed in the span of a week. Scott had hit the nail on the head when he said the new manager would ask for me. Before I had the chance to even glance at my morning emails, he sent me a message to find him in his office.

"Come to my office," it said. No introduction or pleas-antries. It appeared the new manager was a "no bullshit" kind of guy.

Blinds covered his office windows, blocking my view inside. I knocked on the hardwood door, and a crisp "Come in" came from the other side, signaling me to enter.

The person inside was not what I had expected. Nick was pushing his late fifties, and this guy couldn't be a day over thirty. When Scott said the new manager had more experience, I was expecting someone closer to Nick's age, not someone my age. It was very admirable that he was able to obtain such a high position at his age.

"You must be Zack." He finished typing on his computer before glancing up at me. He clasped his hands together in a way that very much reminded me of being reprimanded in the principal's office in high school.

"That's me. I heard you're the new manager. It's nice to meet you—" I glanced at the tiny metal name plate on his desk. Joshua Dean, it said. "—Josh."

He winced like the name grated his ears. "I go by Joshua. I was expecting you back in the office on Friday."

"Sorry, *Joshua.* Yes, I was due back from my business trip on Friday, but I requested time off from Nick since I was moving. He said he would put my request in the system." I wasn't trying to be snide, but this guy just rubbed me the wrong way. He made so many assumptions about me before even meeting me. Didn't he know that when you assumed, you made an "ass" out of "u" and "me"?

"I see." He turned back to his computer, probably checking the system for my request. "I see it now," he said.

"Looks like you found it, great. Is there anything else I can do for you?" I asked.

"Actually, there is. I heard you're in charge of the Lucino

project. You're being taken off of it. Scott will take over for you."

"What?" I exclaimed. "I've been working on that project for months. We're only a few months away from grand opening. Does Lucino know about this?"

Fire burned in my belly. How dare he take me off of my own project just because he wanted to! Could he even do that? Lucino loved me. He had a vision to open his own little Italian café in his later years in life. He and I had been working together for months to make that dream come true.

"He does. He was very understanding after he saw Scott's portfolio. As you know, Scott is an expert in Italian restaurants and cuisine. He should've been the one to get this project in the first place," Joshua explained, like he was speaking with a toddler.

"I specifically requested this project to expand my knowledge and to get out of my comfort zone. Nick knew I could handle it. That's why he trusted me to take care of Lucino." I had done hours of research and visited countless Italian cafés and restaurants in preparation for this project.

I loved a challenge, and this was my biggest challenge yet. Lucino and I planned everything together. From his menu to his decor, we spent hours poring over books and taste-testing his recipes. We were so close to the finish line, yet this jackass pulled me right before I could taste the sweet victory of our hard work. What a jerk.

"I see. I'll take that in consideration for future projects. However, the handover procedure for this one has already been completed. You may return to your work." He waved his hand in dismissal.

I not-so-accidentally slammed the door shut. It was a pity that it was one of those soft-close doors, probably for all the angry people that had left this office in the past. I was sure

Joshua would greatly appreciate the silent closing functions of the door as I was absolutely certain there would be plenty more people coming out of his office in a bad mood in the future.

Scott's head popped over the cubicle wall as I sat down. He looked slightly guilty. "You heard?" he asked.

"I heard. How could you just let him give you *my* project?" I glared at him. I knew he wasn't at fault, but I was in a blaming mood.

He shot his hands up in a defensive manner. "Dude, I tried telling him you could handle it, but he wasn't having it. I tried, man." He deflated. Scott reminded me of a puppy sometimes. I could imagine his puppy-dog ears lying flat in guilt. Some days, his sweetness could give me cavities.

"Hey, man. Sorry, I know it's not your fault. It's just frustrating, ya know. We only had a few months before the grand opening. It sucks that I won't be working with Lucino 'til the finish line." I rubbed the back of my neck. I shouldn't have laid my anger out on Scott when he wasn't at fault.

"It does suck, but I promise I'll do my best in your place. Even if you're not working on it till the very end, I'm sure Lucino would love to see you at the grand opening party." Scott came around the cubicle to give me a pat on the back. "Wanna get drinks and unwind tonight?"

"Nah, I'll pass. I'm exhausted from the weekend. I just wanna go home and crash." It didn't help that I had to deal with the manager from hell as soon as I came back to work on Monday. The workday had just begun, and I was already waiting for it to end.

The rest of the morning went by in a flash. I sent the last email for the morning and called Scott for lunch. The company was nice enough to provide a subsidized cafeteria for us. And since we were in the hospitality industry, we had a wide range of quality foods to pick from. Throngs of people rushed down to the cafeteria during lunch for this exact reason.

It felt like a comfort food type of day, and my go-to comfort food was ramen. The company had sent a team of us to Japan a few years ago for a workshop. There had been an influx of Asian-style restaurants in the industry, and our company didn't want us to lag behind, so they sent us to learn all about Japanese food.

We spent a week gorging on the most delicious foods. My mouth watered at the thought of the Tonkatsu Curry or even a simple bowl of Gyudon. It was heaven in my mouth.

Scott went to the salad bar for his rabbit food. He said he had gained some weight in his thirties and wanted to lose it.

"Hey, Zack. How's it going?" Jenna from HR came up behind me in line. She squeezed into my personal space as she always did, her too-low blouse giving me a grand tour of her plump breasts.

"I'm, uh, good. How are you, Jenna?" I took a step back. She followed.

"I'm great. I missed you last week. I heard you went out of town?" She twirled a strand of her hair, a shy smile spilling from her lips.

Don't get me wrong. Jenna was a beautiful woman, and I was sure most men would be hooked by her cuteness, but she had entirely the wrong set of equipment for me. I just didn't know if she knew that.

I didn't think I could make it any clearer to her. I'd told her on multiple occasions that I was heading to Joe's, our local gay pub. Heck, I even told her once that I was getting dinner with my boyfriend. She replied saying that she loved getting dinner with her girlfriends too.

I didn't know if she was incredibly dense or just delusional.

I hoped it was the former because nothing was more terrifying than a woman who thought they could turn a gay man straight.

She was relentless with her flirting and probably hoped that I would ask her out. Since she never outright said anything, there was never a good time to tell her how gay I was.

"Yea, I just got back into town. Oh, look. They're calling my order. I'll see you later."

"Wait—" I didn't give her a chance to finish. I was usually more patient with her, but I wasn't in the mood today. All I wanted to do was slurp down my ramen.

When I arrived at the table, Scott was munching on his grass, his eyes sparkling. My interactions with Jenna were, apparently, the funniest thing on Earth.

"Shut up," I grumbled.

"What? I didn't say anything. Though you should've seen the death glares our new manager was shooting at you."

"Joshua?" I asked in confusion. What could I had possibly done to piss him off now?

"Yea. He had lasers in his eyes, man. I don't know how you didn't feel his gaze." Scott stared at my ramen like he was a starving rabbit that had never seen food before.

"Dude, just get a bowl. This diet shit is stupid. You look perfectly fine. Don't I tell you how handsome you are all the time?"

He waved my words off. I met Scott five years ago when I joined this company, and he had always been self-conscious about his looks. Every time I complimented him, he had brushed it off as me giving him lip service since I was his friend.

"I'm not just saying it. You are handsome. If you want to diet and work out for health reasons, I'm all for it. But, don't do it because you think there's an issue with your body because there isn't."

He nodded, not saying anything. He always avoided talking about this.

"Anyway, what problem does Joshua have with me now?" I asked, changing the topic.

Scott perked up now that he wasn't the subject of the conversation. "I heard he has a crush on Jenna. Guess he didn't care for you flirting with her."

"I was not flirting with her," I groaned. That was the furthest thing I wanted to do with her. "Is this the reason Joshua has it out for me?" A woman who wouldn't take a hint kept buzzing around me, and my new manager, who hated me, now thought I was his rival in love. Just my luck.

Scott shrugged. "Dude, you should just tell her you're gay. It would make your life so much easier," he said through a mouthful of green leaves.

"How the heck are you supposed to bring that up in casual conversation? 'Nice day we're having. Oh, by the way, I'm gay?' Maybe you should just act as my boyfriend," I joked.

"Oh, you know you wouldn't be able to handle all of this." He gestured to himself, sitting up straight.

"I know, I know. You're way out of my league." I laughed as we joked and bantered the rest of lunch, taking our time with our meal. Scott and I lingered in the cafeteria while most of the other employees cleared out.

The rest of the work day passed uneventfully. I didn't see Joshua again after lunch, thank God. I didn't want more tension today. I was ready to go home.

I'd lived off of takeout while I was moving and unpacking, but I was tired of fast food, and there was nothing in the fridge. The cool evening air blew away the stress that had built up during the day, and an easy smile formed on my face as I biked to the local market near our building.

A black cat lay outside the door. Its head perked up when I

peddled into the lot. Some people considered black cats harbingers of bad luck and steered clear of them, but not me. How anyone could believe adorable fluff-balls were bad luck was beyond me. If anything, people should consider themselves lucky to be allowed into the presence of such majestic animals.

I parked my bike, locked it up, and entered the store. I turned my head at the sound of the cat's meow. It stared at me and meowed one more time before running off. Was I delusional to think the cat was waiting for me before it left? Probably. But I still smiled at the possibility of it. I turned back around and headed toward the back.

Steak was the perfect way to end the day, so I made my way to the meat section. A man turned the corner just as I walked past and crashed into me.

"Sorry, are you all right?" I glanced up and saw the man I'd been hoping to catch a glimpse of all week. There stood Caleb.

FIVE

CALEB

I was, thankfully, able to get off work early today, but I knew today was a rare instance that wouldn't happen again for a while. Tax season wasn't over yet, and my future included many hours of overtime to catch up on all the work that would be coming my way.

Even if I did decide to take the CPA exam, it wouldn't happen until after the busy period, so I had time to carefully think it over.

I stopped by the store near my building on my way home to pick up a few items. Turning the corner back toward the checkout area, I accidentally bumped into someone and extended my hand to stabilize them.

"Sorry, are you all right?" I asked. He looked up, and I was pleasantly surprised to see Zack.

"Funny bumping into you here, literally," I joked.

He chuckled, his deep voice vibrating like a smooth bass guitar. If we were somewhere more private, my pants probably would have dropped for him.

"Yeah, I didn't see you all weekend," he said, the question in his voice.

"I usually go over to my mom's on Sundays. Didn't get home 'til the evening. How is your unpacking going?"

"Almost everything is unpacked. Have you had dinner yet? I was planning on making steak tonight. If you don't mind, you're welcome to join me. It'll be a thank you for the cookies. Oh, I need to return your plate as well." He shifted on his feet.

"You finished the cookies already?" I gasped. I gave him about two dozen cookies, and it had only been a few days.

"My bastard of a friend stole half of them," he said light-heartedly, but the throbbing vein on his temple showed that he wasn't currently happy with his friend for his crimes. His dark expression told me he took his sweets very seriously.

"I can always make more for you later. I bake all the time."

He shot me an earthshattering smile. This must be how angels looked, beautiful and sexy.

"I guess I lucked out getting you as my neighbor. In that case, you have to let me cook for you tonight." I was about to tell him that he didn't need to, but he shot a hand up before I could say anything. "Take it as an early payment for your future desserts," he insisted.

"I...Well, all right then," I conceded.

"Great! My friend Eric is dropping Lady off soon, but what do you say we meet at my place in an hour?"

Who the fuck was Lady? Were all his nut innuendos just jokes? Was my hot neighbor actually married to some girl with a weird name?

"Lady is..." I started.

"My cat. You're not allergic to cats, are you?" Could he get any better? Anyone who loved cats got an A-plus in my book.

"Nope, I love cats. I was thinking about getting one, actually, but I don't know if I have the time to take care of one, and I don't want to leave them home alone all day. Even though they're very independent, I heard they get depressed and lonely if they're by themselves for too long. Some cat owners have video evidence of their cats waiting all day for them by the door, and some studies have even found that cats will get depressed if they're alone for too long," I rambled. I rubbed the back of my head and went back to the topic at hand. "Anyway, an hour from now sounds perfect."

He gave me a smile like he found me amusing. This was why I didn't meet new people. I was the most socially awkward human on Earth. I would be lucky if he didn't rescind his offer of dinner so that he could avoid the rambling outbreaks I had when I was nervous.

Fortunately, he didn't mention my word vomit. We finished our grocery shopping and agreed to meet at his place at six-thirty.

I was so dazed throughout the whole checkout process that I accidentally handed the clerk my ID instead of my credit card. I couldn't stop myself from overanalyzing everything. Did he think I was weird? Why did he invite me over for dinner? Was this a date?

I needed my best friend to break everything down for me. He was the more emotionally adept one, while I spoke of logic and order.

Taking my card back and grabbing my grocery bag, I left the store like a madman. I made it back to my apartment in record time and dialed Ian while I quickly jammed my groceries in the proximity of where they belonged. I could rearrange everything later.

"Hey, sweetcakes. What's up?" Ian's cheerful voice sounded through the speaker.

"Ian! Help! I was invited to dinner tonight. SOS!" My

hands moved around frantically, even though he couldn't see them.

"Hold on, what? Dinner? With who?" He sounded puzzled.

"It's my new neighbor. Can you come up? I need all hands on deck."

"I'll be right there." He hung up and was probably running up the stairs at that very moment. Ian lived on the floor below mine. Even though we had been best friends since high school, he adamantly refused to live with me because he said I was a "clean freak." Just because a man liked his space organized didn't mean he couldn't handle a little mess.

However, he was probably right on that decision. I would go crazy living with his scattered clothes and dirty dishes. His apartment wasn't exactly dirty, but it was clear that he didn't mind putting off the cleaning.

My front door was flung open minutes later, and a flushed-face Ian bounded inside.

"You have to tell me *everything*," he just about squealed.

"There isn't much to say." I feigned calm. "He moved in Saturday, and I gave him cookies to welcome him into the building. He said he wanted to cook for me as an early payment for the baked goods I'd share with him in the future."

"Aww, that's cute," he cooed. "I can already imagine you walking down the aisle carrying a platter of desserts."

I rolled my eyes at his ridiculousness. "Stop it. I don't even know if this is a date or not."

"Who cares?" He opened my fridge and glanced at the contents inside. "Just go with the flow and have fun." His eyes lit up when he saw the brownies I baked the other day. Ian loved sweets as much as I did, and we had many baking experiments at his house when we were younger. Back then, I liked to make my cakes with entirely too much sugar, hence the nickname "sweetcakes." He grabbed a brownie and quickly wolfed it down.

"It's almost dinnertime. Don't you know snacking will ruin your appetite?"

He shrugged and grabbed another one. "I haven't eaten in hours. Anyway, let's get back to the topic at hand. You're not going like that, are you?"

"What's wrong with how I look?" I asked, crossing my arms. I thought I looked very respectable in my suit.

"It would be fine if you were going to audit him, but it doesn't give off 'fuck me' vibes."

"I am not going over to fuck him." I gasped. "He's my neighbor. No, just no. You know how I feel about mixing my personal and sex life. It's weird seeing your one-night stands after the hookup."

He shrugged again and licked the brownie bits off his fingers. "All right, you go jump in the shower. I'll find you something to wear."

"Fine, but don't go overboard. I don't want it to seem like I'm trying too hard."

Ian pushed me into the bathroom. "Don't worry. I got you. Just trust me."

I was slightly worried. The last time he dressed me for a date, though it was months ago, he put me in ripped jeans and a slightly see-through tank that he must have taken from his closet because there was no way I owned something like that.

I put on some shorts and a shirt after my shower and exited the bathroom. I saw Ian standing over my bed, appraising what looked like two shirts. The first was a blue button-up with tiny cats on it that Ian had gotten me as a prank one year. Joke's on him because it was one of my favorite shirts. The second was a more formal white button-up.

"I'll wear the cat one. Zack told me he has a cat."

"His name is Zack, huh? What a darling name." Ian smirked. He picked up a pair of jeans and shoved them at me. "Wear these. They make your butt look delicious."

I grabbed the clothes and went to the bathroom to change. I had changed in front of Ian before, but he's a *very* fit personal trainer, and my "tax season belly fat" had graced me with its unholy presence again this year. He would never judge me, but I still didn't want to be naked in front of him right now.

I changed into the pants Ian chose for me, and he was right. They did make my butt look less flat than normal. I put on the shirt and appraised myself in the mirror. Not too bad, if I did say so myself.

"I'm done." I exited the bathroom and gave a little twirl for Ian.

"See, what did I tell you? Any sensible guy would pounce that ass."

I rolled my eyes.

"Now, come here so that I can fix your hair." He pushed me to sit on my bed and reached out to play with my brown locks. The ends almost covered my eyes at this point. I needed a hair-cut, like yesterday.

"So..." I started. "What am I supposed to talk to him about?"

Ian grabbed the hair gel from the bathroom and continued styling my hair. "What do you mean? Just make small talk or something."

"You know I loathe small talk," I grumbled.

"Tough luck, sweetcakes. Just ask him questions. People love talking about themselves." Ian could make conversation with anyone. He had friends from all age groups that lived all over the world. He was the complete opposite of me, yet we had somehow become best friends.

"Tada," he said as he finished whatever he was doing to my hair. "Have a look."

I went to see his work in the bathroom mirror, eyes widening by what I saw. I looked...different, but in a good way. It was still me, but not. Gone was the, as Ian would call it, "stuffy accountant hairstyle," and in its place was something more modern. I looked...hip.

"Wow. I look good." I turned my head left and right to get a better look at the sides.

"It's what I call an artistic mess," he gloated, obviously proud of his work.

"You did an amazing job. I can't believe that's me," I said.

"You clean up good, sweetcakes. Just go have fun tonight. It'll be good for you. What time are you guys supposed to meet up again?"

I glanced at the clock. "Crap, I need to head over soon." I scrambled around to find my shoes.

Ian was waiting for me in the kitchen with one of my bottles of red wine. "It's rude to go over empty-handed," he said.

I took the wine and froze.

"Why are you just standing there?" He raised his brow even though he already knew the answer.

"I'm nervous." I always had anxiety when meeting new people. I cared too much about what other people thought of me and worried too much to actually enjoy being in the present. It was something I'd been working on since I was a kid, but hadn't had much success at fixing.

Ian knew that I sometimes just needed a push. He dragged me out of my apartment and to Zack's unit. One downside of Ian living in the same building as me was that he knew which one was recently empty and gave me no time to delay the inevitable.

"I don't know if I'm ready for this." Sweat tickled my back.

"You got this, sweetcakes." Ian knocked on the door before I could reply.

"Hey, I'm not—" He was down the hall, already headed for the stairs. He mouthed a "go" and put his fists up like he was cheering for me.

I wanted to follow him just so I could complain to him, but the door creaked open at that moment.

I turned back to face the door, eyes widened, accepting my fate.

SIX

ZACK

A knock sounded as I placed the steaks on the cutting board to rest. Turning off the burner, I wiped my hands and went to welcome my guest.

Caleb stood outside stock-still like a deer caught in the headlights. He looked a little startled and very cute in his button-up shirt with what looked like tiny cats printed all over it.

"Hi," he squeaked.

"Hi," I replied.

He thrust out the bottle in his hands. "I brought a bottle of red for dinner."

"Thanks, it'll go well with the steaks. You came just in time. I just took the steaks off the burner to rest. Please, come in." I realized I was blocking the door and stepped aside to let him through. "By the way, I love your shirt."

"Thanks." A slight blush crept up his cheeks. "I thought you'd like it."

He stepped inside and glanced around.

"I like how you decorated the place," he said.

"Thanks, it's not much, but it's getting there." I considered my apartment to be homey. I didn't have many decorations, but the pieces I did have worked together to give a relaxed feel immediately upon entrance.

I grabbed the corkscrew and opened the wine to let it breathe.

Lady sat on the couch, giving a soft meow to announce her presence to the stranger invading her space. She had made sure to cover the whole place in her scent as soon as I had brought her home, so she probably wasn't pleased to find something not smelling like her so soon after she had completed her scenting mission.

"Is this Lady? She's adorable." Caleb sat on the couch next to her and offered his hand to let her sniff it.

"She's a sweet girl, but she doesn't really like strangers. Don't be offended if she snubs you," I warned. Moments later, Lady proved me wrong by climbing onto his lap on her own initiative. She found a comfortable position and began purring.

Caleb's eyes sparkled with delight. "I guess she's taking a liking to me. It's quite the honor." He smiled, scratching the back of her ear as she leaned into his touch.

Lady must have been able to tell how fascinated her owner was by this man. She had always been a smart girl who could sense my thoughts.

"I'll finish making dinner."

"Do you need any help?" Caleb made to get up, but I held out a hand to stop him.

"Stay right there and entertain the little princess. She'll be pissed if I take away her new friend so soon. Besides, I just have to finish the side dish, and dinner will be ready."

"Well...all right, then. But you have to let me know if I can help with anything." He continued petting Lady. She was basking in his attention like she'd never been pet before. Spoiled girl.

I returned to the kitchen to finish grilling the potatoes I'd seasoned beforehand. The smell of garlic powder and paprika wafted through the air as the potatoes sizzled in the cast-iron pan I'd grilled the steaks in. It wasn't the healthiest meal, but it was going to be delicious.

"Let me get the plates for you." Caleb came up from behind me.

"Thanks. They're in the cabinets over there." I motioned my head toward the correct one. He grabbed two large plates, and I proceeded to split the potatoes evenly between them.

"What happened to Lady?" I asked.

"I guess she's done with me. Apparently, a cardboard box is more interesting than me." He pointed to the corner of the room, where Lady was in the process of trying to stuff her body in a box half her size.

"Typical cat." I chuckled. I had purchased numerous toys for Lady to play with, but she had always preferred the boxes they came in.

I grabbed the plates and transferred them to the dining table I had carefully set. Each placemat contained a fork, a knife, a wine glass, and a cloth napkin folded into the Bird of Paradise.

Caleb followed me, carrying the wine. "Wow, these are amazing," he said as he pointed to the napkins.

"Thanks." I preened. "I learned how to do it while I was studying for my hospitality degree."

We took our seats, ready to dig into the meal. Caleb picked up his fork and knife and cut a small piece of steak. He had slender and elegant hands that didn't match the rough calluses that marred them.

He took a bite of the steak and groaned. I wanted to hear

more, preferably while we were both naked, pressed against each other and sharing body heat. I would make sure he moaned all night long 'til his voice was gone.

"This is delicious," Caleb said, interrupting the explicit fantasy that I should definitely not be having about my new neighbor, at least not at the dinner table.

"Ahem." I tried to calm my body and mind and think about something other than the incredibly sexy man sitting across from me. "I'm glad you like it."

"You said you got a hospitality degree, and your cooking skills are obviously top notch. Are you a chef?" he asked.

I watched him bring his fork to his mouth, and my gaze lingered on his full lips. I forced myself to look at my food instead of continuing to stare at him. I didn't want him to think I was a creep, for God's sake.

Cutting into my own steak, I replied, "No, I work as a restaurant consultant, but I do love serving people. It's one of the main reasons I entered this industry."

"Well, you could open your own restaurant with the skills you have." He switched from the steak to the potatoes, letting out another small groan as he got his first taste of them.

I gulped. "Well, what about you? Your desserts are good enough to buy at a premium. Are you going to open a bakery or café?"

Caleb deflated, and his shoulders slumped. I must have touched on a sore subject.

"Sorry, I didn't mean to make you uncomfortable."

"It's fine." He waved me off, glancing shyly up at me. "When I was little, my dream was to open a bakery. My dad and I used to bake together every Sunday, and I thought it was so cool, creating something delicious out of flour and water." His face lit up as he talked about the past.

"That sounds like a fun time. Why did your dream change?" I asked.

"My dad passed away when I was eleven. I guess my goal changed from a pipe dream to something more practical. So now I'm an accountant." His shoulders sank farther down.

I could guess from his reaction that he didn't like his current job much, but it paid the bills. It sucked how many people out there worked a job they hated because they had no other choice. I was very grateful to have a job that I loved most of the time.

"I think you could do it. I've been the consultant to many bakeries that are successful, and I can say for sure that your cookies are on par with theirs. If you opened a shop, it'd be popular. Besides, Corio City doesn't have many bakeries, so you wouldn't have a lot of competition."

I wanted him to achieve his dream, especially since he had the skills to make it happen. Part of my job was knowing what customers liked, and I knew people would flock to any bakery of his to get those white chocolate macadamia nut cookies.

Caleb gave me another shy smile, the tips of his ears tinged pink. "Thanks. Maybe someday, but for now, being an accountant will have to do." A wistful look shone in his eyes. "I'm happy to know you liked my cookies. The next time I bake, I'll make sure to make extra for you."

The rest of dinner flew by as we indulged in delicious food and great conversation. I hadn't had this much fun with someone in a while.

I could tell Caleb was a bit nervous at the beginning. He had a habit of rambling when he was nervous and spitting out random facts, like how goats had accents and that there were moonquakes on the moon. How we even got to those topics, I had no clue, but I found his rambling to be very endearing.

As he felt more comfortable with me, we began to joke around and tell stories of our college days.

"Eric, that bastard, thought it would be funny to deck my room out in tiny googly eyes while I was gone for the weekend. It was funny when I first saw it, but not so much later, when I would wake up in the middle of the night to go to the bathroom and see tiny eyes staring at me. I swear, those eyes were hidden everywhere. It took me weeks to get rid of them, and I don't even know if I found them all."

When Caleb laughed, sometimes he'd lose control, and a tiny snort would come out. When he realized what he had done, his face would redden, and he'd get shy again. I would then tell him another joke, and the whole process would happen all over again.

After a few hours of talking, Caleb couldn't stop yawning. We had finished the bottle of wine not too long ago, and the effects were starting to show on him.

"I'm sorry. I don't find you boring, I promise. I guess the wine made me more tired than I thought." He lifted his hand to cover another yawn, tiny tears formed in the corner of his eyes.

"Let's call it a night," I said, taking our plates to the sink. He grabbed the wine glasses and followed.

"I'll take care of the rest. Go home and get some sleep." I twirled Caleb around and led him to the door.

"But I feel bad making you cook for me and then have to clean up after me as well," he said.

"It's fine. You can barely stand on your feet. You can make it up to me next time."

"I—" He paused, considering my words, then nodded. "Okay, next time, then. Thanks again for tonight."

He turned around and headed down the hall to his apartment. When he reached his door, he turned back to me, gave me another wave, and then opened the door and disappeared behind it.

Next time never happened.

It had been two weeks, and I hadn't caught a peep of Caleb. I had knocked on his door a few times to ask if he wanted to grab dinner or a drink, but he never answered. I should've asked for his phone number that night. I didn't think it was necessary since we lived right next door to each other, but apparently, it was.

Or maybe he was avoiding me? I didn't know why the thought of that bothered me so much. It wasn't like I wanted to date him or anything. I wasn't looking for a relationship right now, or probably ever, but there was something about Caleb that I just couldn't stay away from.

I kept thinking that maybe I had done something to scare him away or I'd messed up by making him remember his dead father. My mind was a mess. And it didn't help that my new manager wasn't making my life easy either. Needless to say, I wasn't in the very best of moods that Thursday morning at work.

Scott had a meeting with Lucino today, so I tagged along to say goodbye and reassure him that he was in good hands with Scott.

I may not have agreed with Joshua's choice to take me off the project, but that didn't mean I was going to make things difficult for everyone involved. After Lucino's wife of thirty years passed away, the only thing that kept him going was this dream of owning a café. I wanted him to succeed, and to do that, he needed to believe in himself and the person guiding him. And I knew Scott would lead Lucino to success.

After promising Lucino that I would attend the grand opening, I said my goodbyes and headed back to the office. Scott stayed to finish up the rest of their meeting.

Joshua was waiting by my cubicle when I got back.

"Where were you?" he asked accusingly.

"I went with Scott to see Lucino."

"Why?" He furrowed his brows. "The handover was already done."

"Yea, but I wanted to reassure Lucino. He's not someone who opens up easily. I wanted to tell him that he could trust Scott."

Joshua pursed his lips, before saying, "I want you to compile the data on these documents." He handed over the folder he was holding.

"This is intern work." I narrowed my eyes. I had been working here for five years. I should be leading projects, not being given busy work.

"Well, we currently don't have any interns. Besides, you have free time now that you're off Lucino's case." He turned around and walked back to his office without letting me get another word in. My mouth gaped open as I stared at his departing back.

He obviously had it out for me. Otherwise, why would he make me do this when we had plenty of newbies that had entered the company recently? I muttered curses as I punched on my keys to enter the data from the documents he'd given me. The sooner I started, the sooner I'd get it done.

Scott came back right before lunch, as I was finishing the task Joshua had given me. I locked my computer, and we headed down to the cafeteria together.

Jenna and Joshua were standing together by the entrance, laughing and chatting. Joshua was even smiling. I almost believed that he didn't have the ability to smile, but apparently,

I was wrong. I guess what Scott had told me was true, and Joshua did in fact like Jenna.

Jenna turned around and caught sight of me. She let out a huge grin while Joshua glared daggers at me behind her back.

There was no way I was getting dragged in this mess. If Joshua saw me talking to Jenna, he'd make my life more miserable than he already had. They said running away was for chickens, but I didn't give a shit. Call me a wuss.

"I'm outta here," I told Scott. I pretended not to see Jenna, turned around, and busted out of there like my life depended on it. Maybe it had—at least my professional life did.

Scott ran to catch up with me, a shit-eating grin on his face. "I was ready for a good show."

I gave him a light shove.

We had lunch at the café down the street. They had a display case full of baked goods, and I couldn't stop my thoughts from drifting to Caleb again. This was ridiculous. I wasn't some teenage boy with a crush. It shouldn't matter if he was ignoring me. Some people just didn't get along.

Enough was enough. I'd rather know straight-up if that was the case instead of brooding over it all day. I would confront him the next time we met. If he didn't want to be friends or have anything to do with me, that was his problem. At least I'd tried.

I didn't have to wait long.

After a long day at work, I dragged my tired body up the stairs of my building. Once I got to my floor, I fumbled for my keys to unlock my door. Just as I was about to enter my apartment, the door to the unit next to mine opened.

Caleb walked out, his face lighting up into a blinding smile when he caught sight of me.

Maybe he wasn't ignoring me after all. You didn't smile like that at someone you disliked, right?

SEVEN
CALEB

I left Zack's place on a high after what I would consider a successful dinner. Not only was he a good cook, he was funny. He'd made me laugh. A lot. He'd made me laugh so uncontrollably that my annoying snort came out, and that was something very few people knew about.

The days following, however, were a sharp contrast to the relaxing and enjoyable dinner we'd shared. I was thrown back into the unavoidable overtime of tax season and reminded again of why I hated my job. I often asked myself why I was still working in a field I obviously despised.

Because it pays the bills.

It saddened me to think I'd become one of the monotonous gears of the corporate machine. Gone was the starry-eyed little boy who'd chased after his dreams. Instead, I'd become a calculating drone that helped my clients pay the smallest amount of taxes.

After almost two weeks of grueling overtime and not seeing the sun, I was finally released from my drone mode, at least until next tax season.

I hadn't seen Zack since our dinner together. There weren't any more chance encounters either as I didn't usually get home until late in the evening. However, that changed on my first day of freedom from overtime.

It was Thursday, game night. The first year Ian and I moved into the building, we met Will and Jason, who lived in the unit across from mine. The four of us quickly hit it off and developed a friendship over our love of board games. It soon became a weekly event where we got together to gorge on my desserts and bicker like children, as we were all fairly competitive. It was great. It had been weeks since I'd last gone, and I was determined to go tonight and hang out with my friends.

I planned to make cupcakes to bring as an apology for my absence. They were understanding of my job and how busy it got during tax season, but I still felt bad. Only having three people made some board games difficult, after all.

I moved around my kitchen, avoiding the low-hanging cabinets for once, and took out all the ingredients I would need to make the cupcakes. Grabbing the jar I stored my sugar in, I found that I was running dangerously low on the sweet drug. That wouldn't do. What kind of dessert would it be if it didn't have enough sugar? I usually borrowed from Will and Jason if I was missing an ingredient, but they texted our group chat earlier to say that they wouldn't get home until right before the meetup for game night.

I could go next door and ask to borrow some from Zack, but two weeks had passed since we last saw each other. It didn't feel right to ask for something when our friendship was still so new. Besides, the store wasn't that far. It wouldn't take long to pick up sugar and come back. And then I could make extra cupcakes to give to Zack as an apology. I hoped he wasn't too mad about my sudden disappearance.

Grabbing my wallet and keys, I unlocked my door and

headed out. A rattling sound came from my left. Turning toward the sound, I saw Zack in front of his doorway.

I gave him a smile as I walked toward him. He stared at me like he was seeing an extinct animal. His wary expression caused my steps to falter a beat before continuing.

"Hi," I squeaked out, the smile falling from my face. Crap, he was obviously angry at me for basically disappearing off the face of the Earth after our dinner.

"Hi," he replied, his voice holding a hint of gruffness.

"Sorry I've been gone for a while. Tax season kinda kills." I rubbed the back of my neck.

The light came back into his eyes. "That's right. You're an accountant," he said, more as a statement than a question. "I thought you were avoiding me." He seemed, dare I say it, almost sad at the thought that I might have been purposely removing myself from his life.

"Of course not." I rejected his worry. "I enjoyed hanging out with you."

A smile finally landed on his face. He was handsome regardless, but when he smiled, he lit up the world around him.

"I liked hanging out with you too," he said with a cheeky grin, his playfulness back in full force. "Has work calmed down for you?"

"Yes, thank God. Today is my first day without overtime." I shifted on my feet, unsure of how to proceed. "I get together with some guys in the building to play board games," I continued. "We're having a game night tonight. You're welcome to join—only if you want to, of course. I mean, you probably have some other plans already, but if you don't, it would be nice to hang out with you." I forced my mouth shut before I could blabber on. I hated my nervous habit.

Amusement lit up Zack's eyes. "I would love to join. Thank you for the invitation."

"Good. Great! I'm glad you'll be there. I'll stop by at seven tonight to pick you up." I glanced at him, our eyes met, and something sizzled in the air, causing the hairs on my arm to stand up.

"Uh, were you on your way out?" he asked, snapping me out of whatever had just happened.

"I...I mean, yes. I was going to bake something for tonight, but I ran out of sugar," I replied absentmindedly.

"Wait here." Zack left me standing in the hallway. I was dazed, and my body still tingled from the electricity that flowed in the air between us. He came back moments later with an unopened bag of sugar.

"I have an extra bag. Here." He handed it to me.

"Thank you. Let me give you the money for it." I reached into my pocket to grab my wallet. He reached out to stop me.

"Don't worry about it. I'll take my payment in the form of delectable sweets," he joked.

"I'll be sure to make you plenty of extras. Well...I'll see you tonight?" I asked, worried that he had changed his mind in these past five minutes.

Thankfully, he nodded, dispelling the worries circling my mind.

We parted after saying our "see you laters." Now that I had everything, I went back to my apartment to make the desserts I'd promised him.

I didn't know what kind of flavors Zack liked, so I settled on chocolate cupcakes. Who didn't like chocolate, right?

They said that baking was both a science and an art. I enjoyed it as a form of artistic expression, but it was the precise-ness of the whole process that calmed me. It was gratifying to know that as long as I followed the recipe to the tee, I'd be rewarded with a delicious dessert in the end. I didn't have to think about variables or unforeseen incidents, unlike real life. I only had to follow the recipe.

Each measurement of the ingredients was precise. I made sure to scrape off the top of the measuring cup with the backside of a knife to get the exact amount noted in the directions. There were times I tried my own hand at creating recipes, but when I followed one, I made sure to follow it to the letter.

Two hours later, I had three dozen cupcakes—one for Zack and the rest for game night—cooled and frosted. I'd eaten a quick and simple meal while the cupcakes baked and had finished it off with a taste of my newly baked cupcakes, and boy did they turn out amazing.

I packed Zack's share onto a large plate and put the rest of them in a cupcake holder. Leaving the cupcake holder behind, I grabbed Zack's share to drop off at his place.

The TV played soft music from beyond the door. Zack's deep voice flowed through the door as he reprimanded Lady for scratching up the couch. She must have stopped since the only thing that could be heard now was his soothing rumble telling Lady what a good girl she was and all the other sweet nonsense one told their pets.

I couldn't move my hands or feet. I just stood there, listening to Zack's deep timbre, each word a lightning strike coursing through my body. I was addicted to his voice. My body craved to be around him. The slight electricity in the air was a comfort I never knew I wanted.

Who knew how much time passed before I was snapped out of my daze by the mention of my name? Or at least, I think he mentioned my name. There weren't many words that were similar to Caleb, so I was almost certain that was what he had said.

My heart kicked a beat, pounding louder than any human heart should. *Get yourself together, Caleb!* This wasn't the time for me to be standing here and brooding over a man. He was waiting for me on the other side of the door.

Taking a long, deep breath to calm my nerves, I worked up the courage to give a soft knock. He must have been waiting for me as the door flung open within seconds. There he stood, Lady in his arms and a huge grin on his face like he was excited to see me.

"Hi," Zack said, and his green eyes sparkled, illuminated by the hallway light.

"Hi," I peeped out, my voice an octave higher than normal. "Ahem. I mean, hi." I tried again, lowering my voice so that I didn't sound like a kid going through puberty.

Zack shot me another grin, delight dancing in his eyes.

Lady waved her tiny legs around, struggling out of Zack's arms. Zack complied, and Lady landed on the ground with a soft thud. She walked toward me, weaving herself through my legs to greet me. Once she was satisfied, she walked back into the apartment and found a spot on the couch.

We were both silent while we watched her antics. Her presence broke the awkwardness that flowed through the air, and we burst out in laughter.

"Cats, am I right?" Zack commented.

I only managed a nod, my fit of laughter bringing out tiny snorts again, something that occurred often around Zack.

"Anyway, are those for me?" He wiped a stray tear from his eye and pointed at the plate I was holding in my hands.

I nodded again, my laughs finally calming down into a relaxed smile.

"For you." I handed the plate to him, thoughts turning into worries. Would he like them? Did he even like chocolate?

"These look fantastic." Zack took the offered plate and twisted it around to admire my work. "I can't wait to try one. Come in."

He headed back into his apartment and placed the plate on his kitchen counter. He entered the kitchen to wash his hands and dried them before coming back around the counter where I stood.

"Do you want to eat one with me?" Zack picked up two cupcakes and handed me one.

I already knew what they tasted like, as I'd had one earlier, but there was no way I was rejecting his offer.

I watched him take a huge bite of the cupcake, his tongue swiping at the chocolate icing that smeared his mouth. The whole process played in slow motion, and all I could do was stare at him. His beautiful, full lips that glistened with saliva should have disgusted me, but it was strangely arousing instead.

"Oh, wow. These are amazing." He moaned his approval. I wished it wasn't the chocolate goodness that was making him moan like that.

I gulped, turning my gaze away before *something* I couldn't hide stood up. I took a bite of my own cupcake to distract myself from the boner-inducing Adonis before me.

"Hey, you got a little—" Zack pointed to the corner of his own lips. I absently swiped at the area he indicated, feeling my face heat up at what a sloppy eater I was.

"No. Here, let me." He swiped slightly above my lip, his finger stained with traces of chocolate frosting that I must've missed.

"Thanks." I watched as he slowly retrieved his hand and brought it to his mouth. My heart drummed double time inside my chest as I watched him lick at the chocolate he'd wiped off my face.

"Delicious." His voice sounded deeper than normal. He proceeded to give me a wink while he continued to suck the chocolate off his finger.

"I...I..." I forgot what words were. He must have been

flirting with me this time. Even someone as ignorant in the ways of seduction as I was knew that winking was something you did when you wanted to attract another human being. Who the heck needed pebbles? I'd take his wink any day.

Nevertheless, his flirtatious behavior still left me speechless. I hadn't interacted with him enough to know whether or not he was serious or if he was just a natural flirt. He couldn't have been serious...right?

I was used to natural flirts as Ian was the King of Flirts. He flirted with anyone and everyone as a coping mechanism. Maybe Zack did the same.

I kept silent. I didn't want him to know how much his wink had gotten to me. Instead, I shoved the rest of the cupcake in my mouth, this time making sure to wipe away any crumbs and frosting.

"You got everything this time." Zack gave me his signature smirk.

The back of my neck burned from his comment, forcing me to remember what had happened moments before. Heat pooled in my belly and inched down my waist.

I cleared my throat in reply. "We, uh, should get going. They're probably waiting for us. I need to grab something from my apartment. I'll meet you outside." I didn't give him a chance to reply, choosing to hightail it out of there instead.

The heat had spread to my face and splotched the rest of my body, and he definitely didn't need to see that. I hated how easily the pink crept across my body when I was embarrassed, or hell, even aroused.

I needed to splash my face with cold water and pray the blush disappeared soon. I didn't have much hope, though. Submerging myself in an ice bath probably still wouldn't chase away the heat brought upon by Zack.

EIGHT

ZACK

Caleb ran out of my apartment like his ass was on fire. I caught a glimpse of the pink blooming on the tips of his ears. After interacting with him a few times, I realized that he blushed. A lot. And it was too irresistible to not tease him and elicit more color on his skin. I wanted to see if the blush spread over his whole body.

No. Nu-uh. Thoughts like that toward my neighbor were strictly prohibited. Teasing him was one thing, but imagining his naked body flushed with color was a whole other Pandora's box that did not need to be opened.

I was crystal-clear about how relationships and I mixed. We didn't. The most I could offer the blushing man was a night of steamy sex, and what a night it would be, but he didn't deserve that. He appeared like the type of man who would want a partner to create a loving home with, and possibly raise cats. I had the cat, but nothing else.

Clearing my thoughts of anything that had to do with sex and Caleb, I adjusted my pants so they weren't sitting so tightly against my eager-for-action cock. Caleb and I were friends, and that was all we'd ever be. I could get Eric to come to the pub with me this weekend so that I could find someone to release some of this tension with and maybe finally get Caleb off my mind. Unlikely, but one could hope.

I found a cover for the plate of cupcakes so that Lady wouldn't mess with them.

"No," I said in a voice that hopefully conveyed that I was the dominant alpha in our family, not her. "Not for you, okay?"

She wasn't amused. She stared at me like I was cute for thinking I could tell her what to do. Lady did what she wanted and very unapologetically.

"All right, I'll be gone for a bit. Be good." She rubbed her head against my hand as I patted her, and she gave a tiny meow to send me off. I swear she understood what I said to her but had selective hearing and ignored what she didn't want to hear.

I grabbed my keys and phone and left the apartment. Caleb said game night was held inside the building, but I'd just moved in and hadn't met the people living in the remaining two units on my floor yet. I locked my door just to be safe. I didn't have anything valuable enough inside my apartment to steal, except for Lady, but there was no way I was letting some thief steal my precious girl.

The hallway was empty. I half expected Caleb to be out here waiting for me, but he was nowhere in sight. I contemplated if I should knock on his door, but figured he needed a bit of time to situate himself and would be out soon.

I didn't have to wait long. Caleb came out holding a container of what looked like cupcakes. The tips of his hair held droplets of water like he'd recently splashed his face. The thought of him needing a cold splash made me smile. I liked the fact that I got him so worked up that he needed to cool down.

"Hi," he said shyly as he self-consciously pushed his wet locks away from his face.

"Hi," I replied. My smile grew wider at our greeting. It was a simple "hi," but since he always greeted me like this, it was like we had developed a special greeting for each other, and the thought of Caleb and I sharing something that belonged to us brought tiny butterflies to my stomach.

"Uh, we should probably get going." He pointed over his shoulder back toward his apartment and the stairs.

"Sounds good. Where exactly are we going?" I asked.

"Oh, I forgot to mention. Will and Jason are the ones who host game night. They actually live on our floor." Caleb gestured to the unit directly across from his.

He opened the door, not bothering to knock. Inside sat three handsome men. A lean guy with defined muscles leapt up from his seat and shot toward Caleb.

"Sweetcakes, you're finally here." He jumped into Caleb's arms and clung to his body.

A pang of jealousy I had no right to feel shot through my body. The familiar nickname the stranger used to address Caleb didn't sit well with me either. It suited him, but that didn't mean I liked hearing it coming from another man's mouth.

"Ian, you're gonna make me drop the cupcakes." Caleb struggled to get out of his arms. Caleb was a few inches taller than Ian, but his height didn't help him escape. "Gah, why are you so strong? Did you start lifting again?"

"No, not the cupcakes!" Another one of the guys shot toward us. He was what I would describe as the stereotypical twink. His boyish looks fit well with his slight frame and height. He was the smallest one here.

The twink grabbed the container from Caleb's hands and bounded back to the giant sitting by the coffee table.

"Yep, I figured I'd bulk up a bit for the summer. I missed you, sweetcakes. You've been MIA these past few weeks." Ian *still* clung onto Caleb's body, and I had a very strong impulse to pry him off.

"Sorry, you know how it gets during tax season. I'll finally be able to make it to weekly game night, though." Caleb gave him a soft smile. They were obviously close, and another pang of jealousy shot through me. I was being ridiculous. I didn't own Caleb. God, I'd only met him a handful of times. He had his own life and his own friends.

I shook the thoughts off and stepped closer to them. Caleb caught my eye and gave me another one of his shy smiles.

Ian also noticed me and *finally* let go of Caleb. "And the sizzling hotcakes over there must be Zack. Caleb has told me, well, absolutely nothing besides the fact that you're our new neighbor and that you're, and I quote, 'smokin' hawt.'" He dragged out the last word.

"Ian!" Caleb shot a glare toward his friend. He was angry that his friend let slip that kernel of information, but my heart was doing somersaults at the fact that he'd mentioned me to his friends. And he thought I was hot.

"What? That's what you said."

"I...I did not say it like that," Caleb stammered. Ian rolled his eyes at him and approached me.

"Anyway, don't mind him. I'd like to get to know all about you." Ian put his arm around my shoulders. He may or may not have sniffed me a bit. Everything was happening too fast for me to process.

Ian and I were around the same height, but I was broader than him. He might have had muscles, but his frame was still on the leaner side.

"Ian, you're scaring him." Caleb shot me an apologetic look.

Ian let out a tiny harumph and released me. "Fine, I'll keep my hands off your man."

"He's not—" Caleb started, but Ian ignored him and joined the other two men instead.

"Sorry about Ian. He's always like that, so you don't have to take him too seriously." Caleb shuffled at his feet.

Was he feeling as awkward as I was about what Ian had called me? *Your man.* It felt so right, but I knew it was not meant to be. Relationships just didn't work for me. The few times I'd tried seriously dating had left a bitter taste in my mouth. The relationships either fizzled out, or I'd find that I was the only one who understood what exclusive meant. I was better off alone. I thrived alone—or at least, that was what I told myself.

"Don't worry about it." I smiled and prayed he didn't bring up what Ian had said. It was best to ignore it and pretend it never happened.

Thankfully, Caleb didn't look too keen on bringing it up either. He led me to the living room and introduced me to the other guys.

"The one gobbling down the cupcakes is Jason." He pointed to the twink who had a cupcake in each hand. I noticed some cupcake wrappers lying on the coffee table as well. I liked him already. He knew how to live life right by enjoying good food.

"The gentle giant over there is Will." He also held a cupcake in his hand but was eating with a lot more reserve than Jason.

"Guys, this is Zack. He moved into 2B."

"Nice to meet you, and thanks for having me," I said and waved in greeting.

Will grunted in reply before flickering his gaze back to Jason.

"Welcome! You should have a cupcake. Caleb, these are so good," Jason said between bites. He choked a bit from eating too fast. His hand reached out as if expecting something, and Will handed him a glass of water like they'd done this routine many times before. The way they acted with each other felt natural and had a different vibe than how Caleb and Ian acted together. I wondered if they were going out. They did live together, after all.

"Slow down. No one is going to take it away from you." Will had a deep and gruff voice. It was how I imagined moody lumberjacks in those romance novels sounded.

Caleb sat down next to Ian. He patted the space next to him and gestured for me to sit. I squeezed into the space, my fingers brushing against Caleb's, and electricity shot through my body.

His hand shot back at the contact. "Sorry. Static electricity."

"Friends, what are we playing tonight?" Ian asked as he reached forward to grab a cupcake.

"We just stocked up on beer. How about Kings?" Jason suggested. He'd recovered from the choking and was now bouncing on the floor excitedly, probably high on sugar.

"Oh, no we don't," Ian interjected. "Not after last time. You don't follow the rules, and you end up drinking every round, which ends with you getting trashed and puking all over the person sitting next to you, AKA, me."

"The beer was good. It was apple-flavored," Jason said, his shoulders shrinking in a bit. He bounced back up the next second. "But I promise not to do that this time. I'll follow the rules and—"

"Jason." Will interrupted him with a pat on the shoulder. They stared at each other for a second. Jason shot him a pleading look before his shoulders deflated, and he finally stilled.

I swear they'd just had a whole conversation with their

eyes. I didn't think it was actually possible, but I'd seen it happen right in front of me.

"Are they together?" I whispered to Caleb, curious to know what their deal was. Jason apparently heard my question and shot up once again.

"Of course not. That's so silly. Will's my best bud." He hooked his arm around Will and pulled him into a half hug.

A look of hurt flashed through Will's eyes before it turned into resignation. He grunted and shrugged Jason's arm off.

"What?" Jason asked. He tilted his head at the cold behavior.

Will didn't say anything in reply. Ian scoffed and rolled his eyes. I wasn't the only one who could see the strange atmosphere between the two of them.

Caleb blinked his eyes and looked around the room in confusion. At least Jason wasn't the only one ignorant of the situation in the group.

"How about we play a non-drinking game? I have an early client tomorrow anyway." Ian grabbed a card game from the stack of games on the shelf behind him and set it on the coffee table. The cards were split into black and white ones. I'd never played the game before, but it sounded fun when they explained it to me.

And it was fun. We all laughed at the hilarious, and often dirty, combos we came up with.

An hour into the game, it was Will's turn to pick the victor of the round. He chose a card that mentioned something about two dicks and a Chinese finger trap. Everyone cracked up as he read the prompt with his final choice.

I couldn't stop my eyes from straying to Caleb. While Caleb laughed along with the rest of us, his face heated up in a deep blush at the mention of cock. I found that his blush did in fact extend down to his body. When an especially dirty card was played or when he was laughing so hard he turned red, pink would splotch his arms, his pale skin making it easily visible. It made me want to find out what the rest of his body would look like dyed in that color.

My skin prickled, and I glanced over to find Ian's piercing stare. He gave me a knowing look before turning away to listen to whatever Jason was saying.

I wasn't doing anything wrong. Caleb was the only one here I knew, and he was my friend. Friends looked at each other. Perhaps my thoughts weren't very friend-like, but what the other person didn't know couldn't hurt him, right? Besides, who didn't imagine their friends naked, especially when they were as cute as Caleb?

I slumped down, my gaze on the floor. I wasn't fooling myself. I didn't imagine my other friends naked, wearing only their glasses. It was one particular man with a sweet smile that made my thoughts go in that direction.

"Zack, are you all right?" Caleb's soft voice brought me back from my thoughts. He laid a warm hand on my shoulder, his gaze filled with concern.

"Yeah. I, um, I'm just a little tired." I coughed to break the awkward silence. Everyone's eyes were now fixed on me. Will gave me a sympathetic look like we were comrades suffering in unrequited love together. Which we were not, because I did *not* think of Caleb that way. Sure, he was often on my mind, but that didn't mean anything. I just wanted to be his friend.

"Maybe we should call it a night. I'm getting tired too." Caleb stood and stretched his arms over his head. My eyes were automatically drawn to the sliver of pale skin that peeked under the hem of his shirt. Ian caught me staring, and I immediately shifted my gaze.

What the heck was I doing? I was checking out my friend while in front of his friends. I had too much sexual tension built up; that was all it was. All I needed was a good hookup. Then I'd be able to treat Caleb like any other friend.

We didn't stay long afterwards. Caleb and I bid our farewells after helping them clean up the mess we'd made. Ian stayed a bit longer to chat with Will.

Out in the hallway, we both stood there, shuffling our feet.

"Thanks for inviting me tonight. I had a lot of fun." I broke the silence.

Caleb shot me a dazzling smile. "I'm glad you had fun. We have game night every Thursday. You should join from now on."

"I'll be there." He and his friends were good people. They tried to make me feel included and joked around with me like we were old buddies. Will didn't speak much, but I'd learned that he just didn't speak much in general. It had nothing to do with me.

"Well, I guess we should call it a night."

"Yeah," I replied absentmindedly. He turned toward his door, ready to open it and disappear behind it. What if I never saw him again? What if it was like last time? I knew my thoughts were silly, as we were neighbors, but I couldn't get the nagging feeling out of the back of my head.

"Hey." I reached out to grab his arm. "I, uh, forgot to ask you for your number last time. I don't want you disappearing on me again." I gave him a wink, hoping I didn't sound as desperate as I felt.

He laughed it off and reached into his pocket for his phone. "Here, put your number in and I'll send you a text."

I handed it back to him. He typed something on his screen, and moments later, my phone buzzed in my own pocket.

"There, now I can't disappear on you." He gave me a cheeky smile before turning to his door.

"Goodnight, Zack," he whispered, his back to me.

"Goodnight, Caleb." I watched as he entered his apartment. He gave me one last look through the crack of his door before shutting it.

I walked back to my apartment in a daze. Lady sat at the doorway to greet me like she always did. She rubbed herself all over me before waltzing toward my room. I grabbed my phone from my pocket and opened the text message he sent me.

Unknown number: Hi :)

There was nothing remotely sexual about the text, but for whatever reason, I got hard. Images of Caleb's sweet smile and flushed body passed through my mind.

I unzipped my too-tight jeans and released my cock from its restraints. It was red and angry with desire that was completely brought upon by my sexy neighbor. I imagined each time he nervously said "hi" to me and the cute blush that would mark his ears.

I closed my eyes, and a vision of him lying under me appeared in my mind. He was wearing nothing but his glasses. His pale skin illuminated against my dark bedsheets, and I made damn sure his whole body was marked red, either from my mouth sucking on his luminous skin or his blush from my teasing.

I played with the tip of my cock as I imagined leaving purple marks claiming him as mine, the hickeys a stark contrast to his skin. With one more tug of my cock, I sighed in pleasure as cum spurted all over my hand.

My body slumped against my door, and my erratic breathing slowly returned to normal. I softly banged the back of my head against the door and stared at the ceiling. Oh, god. I was in trouble.

NINE

CALEB

I saved Zack's number on my phone as soon as I shut the door. A huge grin was pasted on my face as I thought about tonight. I kept feeling Zack's gaze on me all night. There were times I'd glance at him and see him quickly avert his eyes, a sheepish look pasted on his face.

Ian kept wiggling his eyebrows at me whenever our gazes met. Besides the sparse texts throughout the week, I hadn't had a chance to talk to Ian since the night I had dinner at Zack's place, and I desperately needed to ask him how to navigate this new, strange relationship I was developing with my new neighbor. He'd said Will needed to talk to him tonight. If that hadn't been the case, I would've dragged him back to my place to have a long analytical review. He would grumble about it but would comply because he was a sweetheart that put up with my ramblings and overthinking nature.

I gently banged my head against the door, chastising myself. It didn't matter what Zack thought of me. He and I were never going to happen.

First of all, he was my neighbor, and I had a strict rule to never get involved with those in my daily life. I couldn't even speak properly to someone who once confessed their feelings to me, much less someone I had sex with. Hookups were meant to be with strangers that I never had to see again.

As for ex-boyfriends...They didn't exist. I was either too busy with school, work, or avoiding those who had professed their loved to me until the friendship eventually fizzled away. I know. I was a terrible person. But once they'd laid their feelings out, they stepped out of the compartment I made for them, and I didn't know how to handle that.

I was very much a Virgo. We were said to be very systematic, and I embodied that perfectly. Friends were friends. Hookups were hookups. There was no box labeled "friends that once admitted their attraction to me, but I rejected, and we stayed as friends." This was the very same reason I couldn't imagine being friends with an ex. Honestly, I thought those who managed that were a bit crazy.

And secondly, I didn't even know if Zack had any sort of feelings for me. I was probably making this all up in my head by overthinking everything again. That was why I needed to talk to Ian. He would tell me what was up.

I knew overanalyzing wouldn't do me any good and would just make me go stir-crazy. I made myself a cup of chamomile tea to take to bed. The warm drink relaxed my muscles, and I let out a tiny sigh as I sank into my bed and drifted to sleep.

My blaring phone alarm shocked me awake. I fumbled to grab my phone from my nightstand and turned off the blasted thing. Alarms were a great invention, but they were also terrible.

The screen on my phone read six in the morning. I groaned and chastised myself for forgetting to turn off the alarm I had during tax season. There was usually so much work piled up that I went into the office early so that I didn't have to stay past midnight.

Now that tax season was *finally* over, I didn't have to rush to the office anymore. I threw the covers over my head and closed my eyes, hoping to catch a few more hours of sleep, but my annoying brain wouldn't let me drift off into sweet oblivion. I groaned again and threw the covers off and pushed my wavy locks out of my face.

If I wasn't getting more sleep, I might as well get back into my routine of morning jogs. I washed up, put in my contacts, then changed into my workout clothes and got my running shoes on.

Ian had gotten me one of those phone holder things you put on your arm. He said they were a lifesaver during workouts, and he was right. Strapping it to my arm, I grabbed my wireless headphones and slung them around my neck. I didn't bother bringing my keys since I knew most of the residents living in the building. I didn't have anything worth stealing anyway.

I stepped out into the hallway and winced as I absentmindedly shut the door a little too hard. I hoped I hadn't disturbed anyone's sleep. I didn't hear any movement for a second and thought I was in the clear. However, moments later, Zack's door opened, and his head peeked out from behind it.

Crap. I wasn't expecting to see him again so soon. I hadn't had time to organize my thoughts yet. How was I supposed to act? What was I supposed to say to him?

"Um, hi." I did a mental face-palm. I could've said anything else but that, like wishing him a good morning or something.

Zack glanced away from me, almost guiltily. He cleared his

throat and replied, "Hi." Looking at my outfit, he continued, "Are you going out for a run?"

"Yeah, I was just about to head out for one. Sorry if I woke you." I rubbed the back of my neck in embarrassment. This was not what I expected our next meeting to be like.

"It's fine. I'm an early riser." He shifted on his feet. "I haven't found a good gym near our building yet."

"Oh, Ian works at a gym around here. I can ask him to give you a tour of the place." Zack stared at me, waiting for something, for what exactly, I didn't know. I already told him about the gym near here. Perhaps...

"Did you, uh, maybe want to go on a run with me?" His face lit up with a bright smile once again. I guess that was what he was waiting for.

"I'd love to," he replied.

"I usually run a few miles down to the lighthouse and back. Is that okay with you?"

"Sounds perfect. Let me change and I'll be right back." Zack left the door slightly open as he went to change. Lady squeezed her way through the crack of the door and sashayed toward me. She wove her body through my legs before standing on her hind legs, begging to be picked up like a dog usually would. Weird. I had never seen a cat do that before.

Of course, I complied with her demand. Whatever the lady wanted, right? She nestled her body in my arms and began to purr.

Zack came out moments later, dressed in joggers and a plain tee. He paused when he saw Lady cuddled in my arms. "I can't believe she let you pick her up. She usually only lets me hold her."

"What can I say?" I shrugged. "I guess I have a way with cats."

"I'll put her back in the apartment and then we can get going." He held out his hands to take her. I tried to pull her off my body, but her nails hooked onto my clothes, refusing to let go.

"Lady," Zack said in a warning tone. She must've understood because she let go and obediently went into Zack's arms. "I'll be back soon." He gave her one last pat on the head before letting her jump out of his arms and into the apartment. Zack shut the door behind her. "All right, I'm ready."

We made our way down the stairs and to the boardwalk behind our building.

"I can't believe we live so close to the beach," he commented, starting his pre-workout stretches beside me.

"Yeah, living here is a dream. Ian told me the owner bought the building as a hobby. That's why it's so affordable. You're pretty lucky. The units usually fill up fast, but yours needed some renovations after the last tenant left."

"I am pretty lucky." Zack looked at me when he said those words, a deeper meaning hidden in his eyes.

My skin prickled under his intense gaze, and I coughed to mask my unease. "We should get going."

He put in his earbuds and gestured his hand in a "lead the way" motion. I adjusted my headphones over my ears and played an upbeat song. I started a light jog down the boardwalk, and Zack followed beside me.

Once our muscles warmed up, we picked up speed and continued at a steady pace. I started running with Ian in high school as a way to stay active in my mostly sedentary life and never stopped. I would say I was a pretty fast runner, but I was surprised to find Zack matching my pace without any problems. My legs were longer than his since I was a few inches taller, but he kept up like there wasn't any difference in our heights.

We made it to the beach in front of the lighthouse half an hour later. Not many people loitered around this early in the morning. In fact, it appeared we were alone.

We slowed our pace and eventually stopped at the seating area of the boardwalk.

"I'm beat. It's been too long since I worked out." Zack guzzled water from the water fountain before plopping on one of the benches to catch his breath.

"Nah, I think you did just fine. You were able to keep up with me." I bent my leg behind me to stretch it before doing the same with the other one.

"That's 'cause I didn't want to embarrass myself in front of you." Sweat clung to his golden skin and glistened in the sunlight. My gaze roamed to his face, and he shot me a sly grin. I gulped and averted my eyes.

I took the bench across from him and sat with my back toward him so that he couldn't see the annoying blush that bloomed across my face. Maybe I should jump in the ocean to cool down. He might think I was crazy if I did, but it would be less embarrassing than him witnessing my body's reaction to looking at him.

"You're not wearing glasses today," he said while motioning to my face.

"Yeah, they get in the way of running. I wore my contacts." I self-consciously touched the place where my glasses usually sat on the bridge of my nose.

"You look good. You look cute with your glasses on, but I can see more of your handsome features without them." He threw that bomb out like it was nothing, and I didn't know what to do with it. I didn't reply and lowered my head to hide the blush that was threatening to form.

Thankfully, he acted as if nothing had happened and said, "The lighthouse is a thing of beauty."

I nodded in agreement, not even sure if he was looking at me. "It's one of my favorite places. My dad used to say that lighthouses guide lost souls home." Tears welled up in my eyes as they always did when I thought of my dad.

"You said he passed when you were young. Can I ask how?"

"Car accident."

"I'm sorry." I couldn't see his face, but I could hear the sincerity in his voice. I'd heard those words too many times since my dad's death, but each time, they were laced with discomfort and obvious eagerness to change the topic. I had the urge to see his face. I turned around to look at him, and my breath caught at the genuine concern showing in his eyes. I was going to cry.

"Are you okay?" He stood and came to sit next to me.

I looked away and brushed his words off with a wave of my hand, barely holding back my tears. "Yeah, of course. It was a long time ago. I was just a boy when it happened, and now I'm obviously an adult. Besides, I still have my mom and little brother. The three of us do just fine."

He placed a gentle hand on my shoulder and let me ramble. It was like he knew that sometimes I just needed to get it out.

"Do you want to talk about it?" he asked softly.

The tears flowed down my cheeks like waterfalls. I blamed it on the fact that I wasn't used to seeing such deep concern like Zack was showing me. Sure, Ian knew that my dad's death left a hole in my heart that remained empty even in adulthood, but we never *talked* about it. I think he didn't know how to cope with my scars, and that was okay. That was just how it was. Society expected us to be strong and not break down from our traumas. We persisted so that we could keep those we loved safe.

Zack's face was filled with gentle worry as he enveloped me in his arms and let me cry onto his shirt.

"M-maybe later. Is that okay?" I asked through my sniffles. I looked up to see his face. I needed to see his expression and make sure he didn't answer a certain way because he felt pressured.

"Of course," he answered, his eyes softening. He held my face in his hands and used his thumbs to wipe away my tears. I didn't see any unwillingness in his eyes, and that made me tear up even more.

He pulled me back into his arms and slowly patted my back like he was comforting a child who'd woken up from a nightmare. I leaned into his embrace, his scent filling my lungs. I didn't know how it was possible, but he smelled...warm. Like home.

We were both sweaty from our run, and I was snotty and leaving questionable traces on his shirt, but he didn't seem to care. He let me indulge in his bear hug until my sniffles subsided. The tears that blended in with his sweat eventually dried.

It wasn't until I left his embrace that he stopped the rhythmic pats on my back. I'd never realized how comforting the action could be, and I longed to stay in his arms, but we were in the middle of the boardwalk. The world was waking up around us, and the beach would soon be crowded with people.

"Thanks." I couldn't look him in the eye, choosing to hang my head down instead. Now that the moment was over, the awkwardness of the whole situation came crashing into me, and I feared that I had messed up.

He lifted my chin up so that I was looking directly at him. He wiped off the stubborn tear that clung to the corner of my eye and shot me a smile that could have blinded me.

"Anytime."

A tingle of *something* fluttered in my heart. Heartburn, maybe? Though I hadn't eaten yet, and I wasn't lying down either...

I was never going to figure this out by myself. I desperately needed to talk to Ian.

TEN

ZACK

It was over. I'd caught the feels. And for my neighbor, at that.

Caleb looked so vulnerable while I held him, his head leaning against my chest. Although he was taller than me, he looked so small while snuggled in my arms, and I pulled him closer like I could shield him from the whole world. No, a little voice in my head said that I *needed* to shield him. Protect him. Do whatever it took so he never looked so heartbroken again.

His sobs eventually calmed, and he left the comfort of my arms. I missed him instantly. Maybe he was providing just as much comfort to me as I was to him.

Sure, I hugged my partners during hookups, but it wasn't the same. The feeling of holding someone in my arms without any sexual connotation was, well, comforting. I didn't know if I'd ever had that before. My parents were distant at best before I came out to them, but after...

Those were thoughts that didn't need to be unboxed right now. I forced my focus back on Caleb. He sat basking in the morning sun beside me. The flush he'd developed from crying had disappeared from his face, but it still lingered in splotches on his neck and arms. He blushed every time we met, though I wished I was the one who had elicited those blushes this time and not painful memories of the past.

We sat on the bench for a few more minutes. Caleb's alarm soon rang to remind us that we needed to head back, or else we'd be late for work. The jog back to the apartment went by a lot faster than the one to the lighthouse. Once I figured out how to actually breathe while running, my heart didn't feel like it was going to explode out of my chest like it had earlier. Running had never been part of my workout, but it had done me a lot of good, in more ways than one, and I planned to make this part of my routine.

Caleb and I parted ways outside of our doors. He cast a shy glance at me as he disappeared into his apartment. I rushed through my morning routine after I fed Lady her breakfast and got ready for work as fast as I could. I had just parted with Caleb, but I had the urge to see him again already. It would be nice to leave for work together as well. Oh, god. I was turning into a sap.

I forced myself to leave the building without waiting for Caleb. I wasn't going to turn into one of those people who changed who they were just because they developed a crush on someone. My life didn't and couldn't revolve around one person. I wasn't my parents.

The office was empty when I arrived. Most people didn't get in until nine, and it was still only eight-thirty now. Since I ran out of my apartment without eating, I figured I'd get some breakfast in the cafeteria before work began.

I ordered an egg white omelet and stood to the side for them to make my order. I took out my phone and shot a text to Eric.

Zack: Joe's tonight?

A text came back seconds later.

Eric: Down. Meet you there after work?

Zack: Sounds good.

I stashed my phone away when my order was called. I picked up the tray containing my breakfast and glanced around the room. Eating with a friend was always more fun than eating alone.

When I was about to give up and sit somewhere by myself, my eye caught sight of my new manager sitting alone in the corner. He was scrolling on his phone while he ate his meal.

I'd never gotten the chance to clear up the misunderstanding between us and figured there was no time like the present. Strolling to his table, I gave a light tap to announce my presence before sitting across from him. His face formed into a scowl when he saw me.

"Zack," he said as way of greeting, his displeasure at my arrival clear in his tone.

"Good morning, Joshua." I made sure to use his full name since he disliked the shortened form.

He didn't appear to appreciate my efforts. "There's plenty of empty seats in the cafeteria." The question of why I had sat in the one in front of him was left unsaid.

"Listen, I know we started off on the wrong foot, but I hope we could clear the air between us," I said.

He didn't look impressed. "What's there to clear?"

"Well, Jenna, for starters."

"What about her?" He crossed his arms.

"I just wanted to let you know that I'm no threat to you. I have no desire to be with her," I explained. Hopefully, he would lower his defenses against me after knowing that I wasn't competing with him for Jenna's affection. Heck, I wasn't even playing the same field as him.

"Oh?" He narrowed his eyes, clearly suspicious of me.

"Yea, she's nowhere near my type." I rubbed the back of my

neck. This conversation was a lot more awkward than I'd anticipated.

Joshua didn't look pleased. He sat up straighter in his seat, his hackles raised. "Jenna is a beautiful and kind woman."

"Whoa, I never said she wasn't," I interjected. I thought he would be happy with my comment, but why did it seem like it made him more pissed? It looked like the best way to resolve this little misunderstanding was to come out and tell him my sexual preference outright.

"I'm gay," I blurted before I could chicken out. Coming out to your friends was terrifying enough, but it was ten times worse when it was your direct manager.

"What?" His eyes widened. He looked like a truck had run him over.

"I'm gay," I repeated.

"You...You're gay? Someone like you?" he gasped in disbelief.

"Someone like me?" It was my turn to narrow my eyes.

"You know. With all your—" He gestured to the arms I'd worked my ass off to bulk out. I hoped he wasn't suggesting I was too muscular to be gay. "And you're so—" He didn't finish his sentence and stared at me instead.

His gaze wasn't full of contempt like the ones I'd seen from homophobes. Instead, he looked scared. His naturally fair skin turned an unnatural shade of white.

"Are you all right?" I asked. I didn't want to be known as the guy who sent his manager to the hospital.

"I...I..." he stammered, his eyes shifting around like he was on the lookout for something. "I gotta go." He grabbed his tray and bolted out of his seat, leaving me speechless.

I finished my meal and went back up to my floor. Scott was already sitting in his cubicle and checking his morning emails. I leaned over the divider that separated our desks and said, "The strangest thing just happened to me."

"What happened?" he asked without taking his eyes off his computer.

"I told Joshua I was gay, and he kinda just ran away from me."

Scott's head snapped toward me. "Dude, you told him?" he whisper-shouted.

"Yep, and he just freaked out."

"You think he's homophobic?" His eyes widened at the last word.

I didn't answer right away and considered it. My gut was telling me he wasn't, but his actions said something else. You didn't run away from someone who just told you they were gay because you accepted their sexuality, but *homophobic* didn't fit him exactly either.

"Nah." I settled with, "Maybe he's just having a bad day."

Scott shrugged. "By the way, did you hear? Muse Hospitality is hiring a new regional manager."

"What?" I exclaimed. "They're not promoting someone internally?"

"Dunno. A friend of mine said they were scouting outside talent. Didn't you say they were your dream company?"

They were. Muse Hospitality was the gold standard in our industry. They had branches all over the country, and they only employed the elite of the elites. I applied to them after college, just to test the waters, but didn't pass the first round of interviews due to my lack of experience. My plan was to gain a few years of experience to build up my résumé before applying again. And I had done that. I'd busted my ass to learn my trade and acquired knowledge on all types of cuisines to expand my reach.

"Are you going to apply?" I asked Scott.

"Nah, I couldn't handle all that traveling." He was right. Regional managers at Muse Hospitality basically lived on the road. They were in charge of overseeing businesses all over the region they were assigned to, and there was a high chance the region they were hiring for wasn't near Corio City.

"You should apply, man. You've built up a lot of rep in our industry, and this is your *dream*." I nodded at him absentmindedly and sat in my chair. It couldn't hurt to check out the position.

"Oh, before I forget. Eric and I are heading to Joe's after work. You coming?" I turned on my computer and waited for the thing to boot up.

"I'll be there," he replied, turning his focus back to his work.

I shot a quick text to Eric to let him know Scott was coming tonight, and he replied with a thumbs up. I put my phone away and opened the browser on my computer. It wasn't exactly professional to look at job listings while at work, but I knew I wasn't going to get any actual work done if I didn't check it out first.

I pulled up their website and clicked on their "work with us" button. Like Scott had said, the position of regional manager was available, but it was for a region on the other coast. I would have to leave Corio City, and possibly my cat. With all the traveling I would have to do, I'd feel guilty bringing her. Eric would be more than happy to take care of her, and she was used to him since we had all lived together during college, but the thought of her not being by my side caused a pang in my heart.

I browsed through the responsibilities of the role, and I almost bounced out of my seat with excitement. The role called for long-term contracts with the businesses that I would be put in charge of, and that was something that intrigued me.

The past five years working with my current company led me only to short-term projects where I'd drop in, fix the problem, and then leave. As the years went by, the sense of accomplishment I had once felt after solving each restaurant's issue dwindled and left me unsettled. I now hated the fact that we only provided fixes and not long-term developmental plans.

I wanted to help each business under my management grow and see them flourish. This position would give me that opportunity. Plus, all my current projects were ending this fall as well. This was the perfect time to consider a job change. I knew if I didn't apply, I would regret it in the future.

I had doubts about all the traveling the position would require. Life on the road got old super-fast. Plus, I had doubts if working at this company was still my dream. But there was no guarantee I would get it, and I could treat this as another learning experience.

I typed up a quick cover letter and uploaded my résumé. Everyone at the company kept their résumés updated since some clients liked to see our credentials. It wasn't long before everything was uploaded and my application submitted.

I breathed a sigh of relief. Whatever happened happened. But, with the application sent, I wouldn't have to keep thinking about it.

I closed my browser and opened my emails, ready to answer unread messages from the night before.

The rest of the day passed by in a blur. Several of my projects needed approval from Joshua, so I had visited his office a few times, but he was never there.

"Scott, have you seen Joshua?" I asked after my third trip to his office, only to find it empty yet again. It was the end of the day, and I wasn't going to work overtime on a Friday just because I couldn't find my manager.

"Isn't he in his office? I swear he was just there." He

shrugged.

I sighed. It appeared my manager was avoiding me. I couldn't do anything else but leave the files on his desk and write a note asking him to review them. If he needed some time away from me, that was more than fine with me.

I powered down my computer and packed my things. "You ready?" I called out to Scott.

"Just need to finish this email. I'll meet you there." He waved me off and continued typing on his computer.

I left him to his devices and took the elevator down to the underground garage. Since I'd planned to ask Eric to the pub tonight, I drove my car that morning. The plan had been to grab a few beers and maybe find a hookup, but that plan had gone out the window after the morning I'd spent with Caleb. There was no way in hell I was going to spend the night with someone else when I'd had Caleb in my arms that morning. The thought of wrapping myself around anyone else besides him left a knot in my stomach.

I pulled into Joe's lot and checked my phone. Eric had sent me a text saying he already found a booth. He was the manager of a hotel located near the pub. Therefore, he usually arrived first and had the unfortunate job of finding us a table on crowded weekend nights. Fortunately, he had always been blessed with good luck.

It was packed when I entered the building, being a Friday night and all, but I caught sight of Eric sitting at a booth in the back. I weaved my way through the crowd of people and plopped down in the seat beside him.

"Hey, man." I bumped his shoulder in greeting. "I see you got started without me."

"Oh, I need it after the day I had at the hotel. I swear, the creeps always come out during the full moon." I hadn't even noticed it was a full moon tonight.

"I'll get you another round. Another beer?" He nodded. I shot a quick text to Scott, letting him know we had a booth in the back before making my way toward the bar.

There were no waiters stationed at the tables on Friday and weekends. They helped out behind the bar and in the kitchen instead. I signaled to the redhead, Alfie, who started working at the pub months ago.

He set a beer in front of a customer and finished ringing him up. He then bounded up to me with a notepad in hand, grinning when he saw me. "Hey, Zack. What can I get ya?"

I ordered three beers and some finger food. I knew Scott wasn't going to eat something so greasy, so I asked for a plate of celery as well. Pubs didn't have much in ways of vegetables.

Alfie rang me up and handed me a number stand so that the waiter could find our table. His fingers brushed against my hand and stayed for a second too long to be accidental.

"Well, well. Look who the cat dragged in." I pulled my hand back and turned toward the person who spoke.

Ian leaned against the bar next to me, sipping on his martini. "Careful I don't tattle to Caleb."

"I...We weren't..." He'd caught me off guard in an awkward situation. It was true Alfie and I usually flirted, but that was before. Before Caleb.

He laughed. "You should shut your mouth before you start catching flies. I was just teasing."

"Are you here alone?" I glanced around the bar, hoping to spot a head of soft brown waves.

"You can stop looking. I'm by myself." Ian read my mind and answered the question I didn't ask.

"Are you on the prowl?" I assessed his clothes. He wore a tight button-up shirt and distressed jeans. He'd even styled his hair.

"Mm, but there's only weirdos tonight. Fucking full moon."

I laughed. "My friend said the exact same thing earlier."

"Great minds." He took another sip of his martini and glanced around the pub.

"If you don't plan to pick up anyone, do you wanna join us at our table?" This would also be the perfect time to ask him about Caleb.

"Sure. Tonight's a bust anyway." We weaved our way back to the booth.

"Why, hello there. Who's this tall, dark, and handsome?" Ian sat across from Eric and waggled his eyebrows at him.

"This is Eric, the great mind you mentioned earlier." Eric raised a brow in question. I ignored him and continued the introduction. "This is my neighbor's friend, Ian."

"Your neighbor? Do you mean your Caleb?" Eric shot me a mischievous grin.

Ian perked up with interest. "*Your* Caleb? Do tell me more." He put his elbows on the table and rested his head on his interlaced fingers.

"I...He...He's not my...My..." I sputtered, incapable of forming a simple sentence.

"Chill, dude." Eric smacked my back. "Don't get your panties all twisted up."

"He may not be yours *yet*, but you want him to be?" Ian asked seriously, the fun and games leaving his persona.

"I...Well, yes, but it's...complicated." How was I supposed to explain that I had this primal desire to make him mine, but I didn't have the confidence to keep him? And if I couldn't stay in a relationship with him, then wouldn't a friendship with him be better than starting anything at all?

"What isn't complicated?" Ian snorted. "Listen, if you aren't serious about Caleb, then you better not play with his heart. If you do..." He made a slicing gesture across his neck.

The playful aura he'd had moments before was completely gone, and in its place, intense pressure loomed over me.

"Putting everything aside, I...I do like him. A lot," I confessed.

He must've seen something in my eyes because he softened a bit and relaxed back into the booth.

"I like you, Zack, and I think you'll be good for him, so I'll give you a tip. Take it slow. He's as timid as a bunny. He'll run the moment he's frightened. However, you better not hurt him."

A soft smile unwittingly broke the serious face I had on. A bunny was the perfect way to describe Caleb. I imagined the many times he looked like a deer in the headlights, ready to run. Then I imagined him with white bunny ears and a tiny tail, his skin blending in perfectly with the white...

"Ahem." I cleared my throat to shake those thoughts away before things got extremely *hard*.

"I won't hurt him," I promised. It was the last thing I'd ever want to do to that sweet boy.

A waiter came to drop off our drinks and food. Ian ordered a beer to replace his finished martini, and we munched on the platter of finger food while we tossed jokes around.

Scott found our table not long later, sweat beading his temples. "Sorry I'm late. I—"

He stopped in his tracks when he saw Ian, probably surprised to see a cute stranger sitting with us.

"Scott, this is our friend Ian."

"Hiya. Why don't you sit next to me, sexy? I won't bite, unless you want me to," Ian purred as he patted the space next to him.

I suppressed the laugh that threatened to spill out of me from the sight of Scott's eyes bulging out of his head comically. Scott never talked about sex, or dating for all that matter, so I had no clue about his sexual orientation. He'd never had an issue with coming to the gay pub, but I'd never seen him flirt with anyone here either.

"You okay there, buddy?" My touch shook him out of whatever daze he was in. He tentatively took a seat as close to the edge of the booth as he could and pulled on his button-up so it didn't stick so closely to his body. Poor guy. He probably felt intimidated sitting next to a hot stranger. He always complained about hating how noticeable his belly paunch was when he sat down.

I was about to offer to switch seats with him when Ian scooted closer and slung an arm around him. "Aw, did the full moon crazies get to you too? Don't worry, us sane people will stick together."

Ian slid a beer to Scott and held his own glass up in a cheers gesture. A tiny smile cracked across Scott's face as he picked up his beer and clinked his glass with Ian's.

Conversation picked back up as Eric relayed stories of the weird requests he'd gotten today at the hotel he worked at, like how a group of adults had requested twenty pillows to make a pillow fort or the one guest who asked if their horse could stay in the hotel room. Ian interjected with his own stories, and Scott chilled out enough to make occasional comments.

As for me...My thoughts drifted back to my conversation with Ian. I'd made it sound like I was going to pursue Caleb, but was that the right thing to do? After all the broken relationships in my life, starting with my parents, I'd given up on hoping for something more.

But things felt different with Caleb. Maybe I could trust him. I would do everything I could to see where this new relationship—be it friendship or something more—could lead.

Maybe I'd caught the full moon crazies as well.

ELEVEN
CALEB

Zack was gone by the time I finished breakfast and was ready to leave for work. I knew this as a fact. On my way to the elevator, I leaned my head against his door like a creep but couldn't hear any movement inside. I left the apartment slightly disappointed that I hadn't gotten a chance to see him again before work. It was stupid since I'd seen him less than an hour ago, but I liked being around him. It felt safe and comfortable.

Now that tax season was over, work had calmed down significantly. Since I wasn't bound to my desk anymore, I texted Ian to ask if he wanted to grab lunch. He didn't work on Fridays and agreed to meet me at Sunrise Roast, a popular café a short drive from my office.

Ian was still on his way when I pulled into the parking lot, so I waited in the car for him. Fiddling with my phone, I finally unlocked it and pulled up the message thread with Zack.

It was short, as there was only one message on it. It was from me. Zack had never replied to my hi, but he'd been with me when I had sent the message, and I saw him the next morning, so logically speaking, there was no need for him to reply. My mind wasn't in a logical place right now.

I debated on whether or not I should send him a message to thank him for what he'd done this morning. Maybe ask him what his favorite dessert was so that I could bake it for him.

I started typing, then immediately deleted it. I tried again, but everything I typed sounded stupid, and I ferociously hit the backspace again.

I stared at the message thread in a daze, the smiley face I sent him mocking me. It shouldn't be this hard. I was just sending a message to a friend. And Zack was...Was he a friend? It didn't feel like he belonged in the same category as Ian and the others. He didn't fit in any of the boxes I had for the people in my life.

Emotions were complex equations that oftentimes puzzled me. The hookups I'd had in the past were mostly quick and detached, a way to let off some steam. And after the deed, the urge to run always blazed through me. The thought of awkward post-coital conversations terrified me, and so I usually bolted before such conversations could occur. I'd never seen a hookup again after our one night together.

Ian had reprimanded me numerous times on my, as he called it, "hit-and-hop" routine. It wasn't healthy, and I understood that. I did. My heart did, anyway, but my mind wouldn't stop running a hundred miles a second until I got the hell out of dodge.

It was fine. I was still in my twenties. I had plenty of time to normalize being in an emotionally involved romantic relationship to myself. I would learn eventually. Probably.

A knock on my window had me jumping out of my seat. Ian stood outside waiting for me. He stepped back so I could open the door and exit the car.

"Sweetcakes, I've missed you." He pounced on me and held

in me in a firm hug. Who needed romantic relationships when I had friends like Ian?

"I just saw you last night," I teased him. Although I'd missed him as well. It had been a while since the two of us had a chance to sit down and catch up with each other's lives.

"You know it's not the same." I did. He gave me one last squeeze before letting me go and settled with hooking his arm through mine. "Let's go before all the tables are filled."

We made our way inside. Thankfully, the lunch rush hadn't arrived yet, so we didn't have to wait long to order. I always got the avocado wrap when I was here. Call me basic, but avocado was a superfood that was filled with nutrients. Plus, it was delicious.

Sunrise Roast had one of those display cases filled with baked goods by the register. It was usually filled with unique pastries I'd never seen in other places before. I always made sure to pick one out to try as inspiration for my own creations.

Since there wasn't anyone waiting in line behind us, I took my time browsing through the selection they had on display today.

The man behind the register saw me looking at them and spoke up. "You should try a dessert while they're still here. We may not have them for much longer."

My head shot up toward him. "What do you mean? You won't be carrying desserts in the future?"

The man shrugged. "The owner of the bakery we source them from is thinking about retiring. She doesn't have a successor, so they're shutting down. She said it wouldn't be 'til the fall, but I'm already looking for other vendors. Unfortunately, the other bakeries around here don't have a very good reputation. I'd rather not sell anything at all if it means having to put subpar products in my café."

"What a pity. Every dessert I've had here has been spectacular." There was something new each time I ate here. I'd created my own recipes before, but they were nowhere near this baker's level.

Ian popped up from behind me and chimed in, "Would you consider contracting from an individual? My friend Caleb here makes pastries on par with what I've had here before."

"Ian!" I half-shouted. I pulled on his shirt to get him to stop talking. "No, I'm not...I just—"

Ian cut me off and thrust his phone in front of the man to show him pictures of some of my creations. "He makes these blueberry cheesecake bars that are to die for."

The man took the phone and flicked through the pictures on the social media account Ian had dedicated to my desserts.

"Wow, these look amazing. Novel as well." He handed the phone back to Ian and turned toward me. "Are you in the business?"

"No, uh, it's just a hobby," I said self-consciously.

He pulled out a card from behind the counter and handed it to me. "Well, if you ever decide to go into the business, give me a call, and we can see if your pastries are a match for our café."

I took the card he presented, still dazed at his offer. Glossy letters were printed on the middle of the card.

Sunrise Roast, Oliver Shaw, Proprietor.

Oh, shit. The owner of this café had just handed me his card and wanted to talk about a potential future working partnership. My dream of opening a bakery and sharing my desserts with others flashed before my eyes. But, it was too risky. I had to support my family. And opening a business needed a lot of capital that I didn't have.

A million thoughts flowed through my mind, still unable to process what was going on. Ian ordered for the both of us while I was still in my mental fog. He paid for the food and grabbed our number stand, then guided me to a random table and pushed me down into the seat.

"I'm going to get my CPA," I blurted.

He scowled. "You hate what you do."

"That may be true, but it's a stable job, and my family—"

Ian cut me off, like he always did when he felt that I was acting stupid. "Your family is fine. Didn't you say Conner got a full-ride scholarship to Marna University?"

"He did," I answered with a smile. I was so proud of Conner. He got a full ride to one of the most prestigious private universities in the country. What's more, Marna University was located in one of the boroughs of Corio City, meaning he wouldn't be far once he left for college.

"And your mom just got promoted to lead waitress at the diner, so you don't have to worry about her either."

"What? She did? How come you know this and not me?" She hadn't told me anything about a promotion. I made a mental note to give her a call tonight after work.

He shrugged. "I had breakfast at the diner this morning. Guess she didn't get a chance to tell you yet. Anyway, my point is that they don't need you to continue sacrificing yourself to support them. They'll be okay. It's time for you to start living for yourself."

"I don't know." I hesitated. "There is a lot going on right now, and there's so much to consider. Honestly, it's kinda stressing me out."

"Is one of those stressors your new neighbor?" A sly smile formed on his face.

Ian always knew what was on my mind. It had been like that since the first time I met him in high school. He was the cool and rich kid while I was the awkward nerd from a poor family who didn't have a dad. And even though his family had money, he wasn't stuck up like the other rich kids in school. He sat in front of me in our Language Arts class. He was the only openly gay boy in our school, and I desperately wanted to be his friend.

I don't remember why, but I quoted Jane Austen to him during our first conversation. He'd smiled in reply and told me we were going to be best friends. He had been right. More than ten years later and we were still as thick as thieves.

"Maybe," I replied sheepishly. "I told him about my dad's death, and he just...I don't know. I felt so comfortable around him that I kinda bawled on him."

"You cried *on* him? Poor guy. You're all snotty when you cry."

"Hey!" I slapped his arm. "You're supposed to be my friend, thus on *my* side."

"I am your *best* friend, and that's why I tell you the truth," he huffed out. "Besides making you feel comfortable, what do you think about him?"

"I...I don't know, but he's always on my mind. What do you think that means?"

Ian gave me a knowing look but didn't say anything. It was a full minute before he spoke. "You should hang out with him more. Get to know him and see where it leads."

"But what if it does lead to something and we start dating, but it doesn't work out because I find out he's an international spy, and we break up? Then I'll be living next to my ex *and* an international spy. I mean I would've been living next to a spy either way, but I wouldn't have known. Everything will be different after I *know*. I'll have so much anxiety that I won't be able to leave my apartment!" I threw my hands up to emphasize my point.

"Caleb, I love you, but you can be such a drama queen sometimes." He rolled his eyes at me, used to my nonsensical ramblings. "You live so much in your head, creating all these what-if scenarios and ridiculous endings to the scenarios that you often forget to actually *live*. Stop thinking so much for once and go with the flow. Let things actually happen before you decide how it's all going to end."

He was right, of course. I over-thought anything and everything. There had been a baking club in high school that I had wanted to join, but I wasn't out at that time, and there weren't any other guys in the club. I couldn't stop thinking of all the ways other students could find out I was gay if I had joined the club and the stares I would get at school once everyone knew. Sure, Ian was openly gay, but he had a bubbly personality that made others not care about that fact. I, on the other hand, was shy and quiet. Being the weird kid was already bad enough, but to add on the title of *gay*, I wouldn't have been able to handle it. I scared myself so witless that I chickened out and stayed far away from the club.

A waitress came out with our food at that moment, saving me from having to reply. I was starving after that conversation and dug into my wrap with relish. Ian was more refined with his sandwich.

"So, what did you have to talk to Will about last night?" I asked casually after gulping down more than half my wrap.

He narrowed his eyes at me, fully aware that this was my attempt to change the topic but went along with it anyway. "He wanted to talk to me about Jason."

"What about Jason?"

"Oh, you know. The usual." I didn't know. To my knowledge, Will and Jason were fine. Last night, they'd acted the same as always. Well, except for when Will shrugged Jason's arm off of him, but maybe he was just hot or something. Will didn't speak much, and he was one of those stone-faced dudes that never showed his emotions, but he wasn't the type to hold a grudge. Especially if the person who made him mad was Jason. I'd never seen him be mad at Jason for long.

"Is everything okay?" I asked, concerned that this was the one time Jason did something to actually make him angry.

"Of course. He just wanted to talk." He waved his hand in a dismissive gesture.

"Let me know if there's anything I can do." I wasn't convinced. Ian changed the topic too fast, indicating that there was more to it than he was letting on.

He grinned and used a finger to smooth out the frown between my eyebrows. "Stop worrying. Everything is fine."

"Okay," I said and let out a sigh of relief. If he said everything was fine, then it was. Ian might leave some things unsaid, but he never lied to me. He wasn't the type to say, "I'm fine," when he wasn't. Though he *was* the type to keep things bottled up and then need time alone to decompress. At that point, the only thing I could do for him—the only thing he would let me do for him—was bake his favorite dessert, leave it outside his door, and do a ding-dong-ditch. When Ian wanted to be alone, he meant it. He refused to see anyone.

Sensing that he was done with this topic, I switched to another one. "So, are you still hooking up with Dean?"

"That narcissist? Hell, no. Being hot and having a huge dick did not automatically make him great at sex. He had the audacity to roll off me as soon as he was done and leave me to take care of myself. What the fuck is wrong with people today? No courtesy at all." For the rest of lunch, Ian proceeded to tell me about all the selfish men he'd hooked up with lately. I laughed at some of the stories and cursed with him at others.

Ian might call me a drama queen, but he had a bit of queen in him as well. That was part of the reason why we were best friends.

The next morning, I refused to get out of bed 'til the sun was high in the sky. It was the first Saturday in a while that I didn't have to work overtime, and all I wanted to do was relax. My grumbling stomach eventually forced me out of bed to feed it. Although it was technically lunchtime, I didn't want to cook and made myself a bowl of cereal.

I never ended up texting Zack to thank him yesterday, so instead, I'd bake him something and thank him in person. He did say he loved my desserts, so I thought that gesture would make him happy. It wasn't because I wanted to see him. Nope, not at all. The only reason I was going over was to thank him. Yep, that was it.

I wasn't fooling myself. I hadn't been able to get Zack off my mind all day at work yesterday. The words Ian had told me rang true. I did live too much in my head instead of in the real world. I prematurely ended things because I was so scared of an outcome that *might* happen.

No more. I was going to take a page from Ian's book and just go with the flow. I was going to shut off my brain and do what my gut wanted me to, or at least I'd try.

After Ian mentioned my cheesecake yesterday, I had the urge to recreate a recipe I'd found recently: white chocolate raspberry cheesecake. My mouth watered just thinking about it. I'd picked up everything I needed after work yesterday, and I lined up all the non-perishable ingredients on my counter, ready to go.

I counted the Oreo cookies I'd need for the recipe and crushed them in the food processor to make the cheesecake crust. Thank the packaging gods for having the insight to put more than twenty cookies in a pack because I may have munched on one or two or ten of them while I worked.

The raspberry sauce was next. I cooked the frozen raspberries on the stove with the sugar. Once it had thickened, I took it off the stove and strained it to make sure everything was smooth. The white chocolate also needed to be melted. I took the creamy chocolate and added the rest of the ingredients, layering the cheesecake before putting it to bake.

Baking was easy. It was one of the few times I could turn off my brain from my countless thoughts since all I had to do was follow the instructions, and the outcome I desired was guaranteed to be achieved. Why couldn't life be like that? Was there a recipe on "how to life" on the internet that I hadn't found yet? Because there needed to be one, like, yesterday.

I hopped in the shower while the cheesecake baked. It needed about fifty minutes, leaving plenty of time to make myself presentable.

I imagined Zack's face lighting up when he saw the dessert I'd made him. He would give me the easy grin he often had on his face. He'd probably want to dig in right away and even offer me a piece. Remnants of the Oreo crust would litter the corners of my mouth, and Zack would use his thumb to wipe them off for me. He'd then bring his fingers to his mouth and lick the crumbs while giving me a sexy wink.

The warm water felt too hot on my burning skin. I turned the water as cold as it could go, but all that managed to do was stimulate my already sensitive skin. Lust shot through my veins, and my dick stood to attention. The cold water did nothing to cool down the fire raging underneath my skin.

Lubing my hand with body wash, I started a slow stroke on my cock. My balls strained each time my hand brushed over the tip and intensified the pleasure flowing through me. My other hand reached down to cup my balls before traveling back to rub against my taint. I wanted more.

I sucked my middle finger in my mouth, making sure it was

thoroughly covered in saliva, and slowly breached my twitching hole. It had been a while since I played with my asshole, and the tightness around my single digit was proof.

I imagined Zack taking his time opening me up and teasing my pucker until I was writhing in agony and begging to be filled. I'd never had shower sex before, but Zack would make it work. He'd push my chest against the wall and pound me into the tiles. My legs would lose their strength eventually, and then he'd turn me around and hold me up with his powerful arms, his pace never faltering.

My finger moved in and out of me as I imagined Zack's cock doing the same, slow and deep. I stroked my prostate one last time before my breath hitched and I screamed out an intense orgasm that left me shaking and leaning on the shower tiles for support. My dick pulsed once, then twice before finally settling down. Air filled my lungs as I gasped for breath.

My heart hammered in my chest as the guilt hit me. *What the heck was I doing?* How was I supposed to face Zack after masturbating to thoughts of him pounding me? It was going to be awkward as fuck.

I let the cold water cascade over me, praying it would cool me down and wash away my guilt like it did my sperm.

Another million thoughts rolled through my mind, and I had half convinced myself to leave the dessert outside his door for him to find. A mini-Caleb sat on my shoulder whispering all the things that could go wrong with seeing him and the humiliation I could face. A mini-Ian sat on my other shoulder yelling at me not to conjure him into my mind while I was naked and to just stop thinking. Period. *Go with the flow.*

He was right, because it *was* weird that an imaginary Ian sat on my shoulder while I was naked in the shower. But also because I truly did need to stop living in my head. I missed out on so much because of my worries and timid nature.

But no more. I was going to march over there and person-ally hand over the cheesecake like I hadn't just been imagining his cock in my ass.

It was hours later when the cheesecake was finished baking and had fully cooled. I didn't want to look like I was trying too hard, so I picked one of my casual weekend outfits to wear.

Wielding the cheesecake as my choice of weapon, I stood outside of his door and knocked. I got this! I wasn't going to be weird about it. I was going to say something witty and act casual.

Zack opened the door moments later, shirtless. Water droplets dripped from his wet hair and landed on his chest. My eyes followed the droplet as it slid down his golden skin, reaching his sculpted abs and down his happy trail to...

"Ahem." My head sprang up at his cough. I stared at him in shock at being caught ogling.

"Um, hi." Goddammit. So much for being witty.

TWELVE

ZACK

A knock sounded on my door just as I was getting out of the shower. I turned around to grab my towel and almost tripped on Lady, who of course was snuggled on top of the sweaty clothes I'd thrown on the bathroom floor after my workout. She was a weird one, but I loved her.

I did a quick dry off and threw on some loose shorts from my pile of clean laundry. I didn't bother with a shirt since I hated the feeling of clothes on wet skin.

Caleb stood outside the door, holding a container of what looked like some kind of cake. His eyes strayed down my chest and lingered at a certain area. I cleared my throat to get him to divert his attention before his stares completely woke up my already excited dick.

"Um, hi," he said, pink blooming across his face.

I groaned internally. At this rate, I was going to get hard every time I saw pink.

"Hi." I feigned nonchalance even though I was anything but calm. He thrust out the container in his hands and shoved it toward me.

"I made you cheesecake as a thank you. You know, for yesterday." He didn't look at me when he spoke, and I had the urge to lift his chin so I could see clearly how much I made him blush.

Instead of doing that, I said, "You didn't have to, but thank you. I can't wait to eat your sweets."

"Ngh." He made a strangled sound at the back of his throat, his face flushed a deeper red than before. "I, uh...I mean now that you have the cheesecake, I should um...I should go. Okay, bye." He turned on his heels to flee. I was faster, though, and caught a hold of his arm before he could escape.

"Wait," I called out, a bit of desperation laced through my voice. "Don't go."

He turned back to stare at the place where my hand gripped his arm. I quickly dropped his arm like it was a hot potato.

"If you're not busy today, would you like to come in? We can snack on your cheesecake and watch movies. Plus, Lady misses you." That was a lie. I was the one who missed him. Lady probably didn't give a rat's ass about anything else besides my stinky shirt right now, but if it made him stay and hang out with me, I was more than willing to put that little white lie out there.

"I...Well." He rubbed the back of his neck with his hand. I slumped my shoulders, preparing for his rejection. Instead, he surprised me.

He did a cute little shake of his head, then faced me with a look of determination. "You know what? I would love to."

My insides did a little happy dance as I led him inside my apartment.

"Go relax on the couch and find a movie. I'll put on a shirt." I grabbed the first shirt I found in my room, then headed to the kitchen to serve us our desserts. I open the lid of the container and cut two generous pieces of cheesecake. I transferred the slices onto plates and grabbed forks for both of us.

"Do you want anything to drink?" I asked Caleb as I delivered the plates to the coffee table.

"Water is fine." I walked back to the kitchen and filled two glasses of ice water. I made sure to close the lid of the container so that Lady wouldn't get into the food, then joined Caleb on the couch with our glasses.

"Thanks," he said, taking the offered glass. He took a deep gulp, his Adam's apple bobbing as he swallowed.

I forced myself to look away. "Uh, so did you find anything you like?"

"Yeah, how do you feel about superhero movies?"

A thrill of excitement at the thought of having something else in common with him energized me. "I love them. Who doesn't love watching sexy men defend the world?"

Caleb perked up, his eyes sparkling. "Right? When I was younger, my room used to be covered in Superman posters, but my favorite movie series now is Thor."

"It's Loki, isn't it? He's such a sexy bastard."

"Yea, I love how the actor portrayed him. Plus, I've always had a thing for guys with black hair." His gaze flicked to my black waves, before darting to the TV. "I, um...Anyway, should we, uh, watch the first movie?"

I bit back a smile, ecstatic to know that I was his type. I didn't dare tease him about it, though, in case he fled in fright.

"Let's do it." Caleb hit play and picked up his cheesecake. I followed suit.

"Oh, my god. There's a party in my mouth. This is delicious." I couldn't stop a small groan from coming out.

Caleb bit his bottom lip and tilted his head in shyness. "I'm glad you like it," he said in a soft voice.

"More than like—I love it. I could eat the whole thing by

myself." I took another bite, not wanting to put my fork down. "You should consider opening a bakery. As a consultant in this industry, I'm telling you that you would succeed."

"You think so?" he asked shyly. "I was talking about it with Ian yesterday. The supplier for Sunrise Roast is retiring, and Ian showed him my desserts. The owner of the café gave me his card and told me to call him if I ever go into the business."

"You must be talking about Osona's place. I was the one who connected her with Sunrise Roast. I didn't know she was retiring. Do you know what she's going to do with the place?" It was a shame Osona was retiring. She was getting on in years, but her pastries were out of this world.

Caleb took another bite of his cheesecake and shrugged. "Oliver, the café owner, said she was shutting it down."

A tiny ball of jealousy burned in my belly at the thought of Caleb knowing the café owner well enough to be on a first-name basis with him. I ignored it and reminded myself that this was good for him. I put my plate down and carefully grabbed both his shoulders so that he was facing me. His eyes widened at my sudden action. "Caleb, you should open up a bakery. Osona is an amazing lady. If we talk to her, I'm sure she'll work out a deal with you. Think about it. You could make your dream come true."

He shook his head. "I...I can't. I have responsibilities, and even if I didn't, I wouldn't have that kind of capital."

"There are grants for first-time business owners, and they have low-interest loans for small businesses as well. We could do the research and make it happen."

His eyes softened at my words, but he still gave me a slight shake. "Thank you. I appreciate you, but even if I do decide to open a bakery, it can't be right now. My family still needs me. I...I can't take such a huge risk."

A hint of sadness lined his eyes, but they were also filled

with resolution. He truly believed what he said. He was willing to give up his dream because he thought the stakes were too high.

I wanted to help him and tell him that this wasn't a losing risk. I would start researching tonight and come up with a business plan to show him.

I nodded and let go of his shoulders. He put a hand on mine. "For real, though. Thank you. It...It means a lot that you care so much."

I gave him a cheeky grin, knowing that he wasn't going to be persuaded tonight. "Anything to eat your desserts."

He cracked a smile at my words. We didn't say anything else as we focused back on the movie. We didn't speak much throughout the movie, but it was a comfortable silence.

Halfway through, Lady came waltzing out of the bathroom and hopped into the space between Caleb and me. And when Lady was beside me, I couldn't help but pet her. With my eyes focused on the movie, I reached out to her, but accidentally petted the back of Caleb's hand instead. While the palms of his hands were roughed with calluses, the back of them were surprisingly soft.

He flung his hand away so fast that Lady gave him one of her "stupid hooman" stares.

"Sorry," I said, though I wasn't feeling sorry at all. I'd grab his hand again if I could.

He shook his head. "Sorry, I overreacted."

I shot him another grin. "No worries."

We spent the rest of the movie with our hands on Lady's back, our fingertips almost touching. Loki might have been sexy, but he couldn't hold my attention while I had a sweet, blushing Caleb next to me. I wanted to reach out that final inch and connect our hands, but I knew it would startle him, so I settled for covertly staring at him from the corner of my eye instead. Creepy? Maybe. Did I give a shit? Nope.

When the movie finished, Caleb stood up and stretched his arms over his head. My eyes automatically locked onto the pale skin peeking out from underneath his shirt. I noticed that he didn't have a happy trail.

I turned away before he caught me staring. I grabbed our plates and took them to the sink. Caleb followed behind me with our empty glasses.

"Thanks for having me over. I guess I should—"

"Do you want to stay for dinner?" I cut him off. Like hell I was letting him leave that easily. "I made Masala pasta for lunch and have a lot of leftovers."

"Oh, I don't want to be any trouble..."

"No trouble. In fact, you would be doing me a favor. Eating by myself gets lonely. Lady is good company, but she's a terrible conversationalist."

He chuckled. "I bet. If you're sure..."

"I am," I reaffirmed. "I'll heat up the food if you wanna help set the table. The plates are in there." I pointed at a cabinet.

It wasn't long before the food was heated up and we were sitting at the dining table for our meal.

He took a bite of his food, and I just watched him like a creep.

"My god, this is delicious." he said as he continued to shove more food into his mouth. I loved watching people enjoy the food I cooked for them. It made me feel like I'd accomplished something big, and a smile naturally filled my face.

"I'm glad," I said, picking up my own fork and digging in.

"I'm gonna have to run more to burn off all this food," he said in between bites. He was one of those eaters who showed how much they enjoyed what they were eating. He was so enthusiastic about his food that it just made you want to eat along with him.

"I was thinking the same thing. Maybe we should go jogging again together? Say, tomorrow?" I asked as casually as I could despite my heart doing somersaults in my chest.

"Sounds good. But I usually swing around my mom's place on Sundays, so we'd have to go early. That okay?" He continued to eat the pasta with relish.

"Good with me." I took a bite of my own pasta, not to be outdone. "Do your mom and brother live near here?"

"Yeah, they live about thirty minutes away," he answered. "I'm lucky I found a job near home. I couldn't imagine going weeks without seeing them."

"You guys seem close. Must be nice." I tried to suppress it, but he must've heard the tinge of longing in my voice.

"What about you? Are you not close with your family?" He stopped eating like it was his last meal and placed the fork down onto the plate to scrutinize me.

"We're not close." I shrugged. I guess that was better than saying that my parents didn't, and hadn't ever, wanted me. "They don't live in Corio City, so I haven't seen them in years."

His eyes softened. "I'm sorry," he said, his eyes holding mine for the first time without a hint of wanting to look away in embarrassment.

"It's not your fault. Besides, it's been years." I waved him off. I didn't want to bring the mood down. Not when I finally had him alone again. Talking about my loveless childhood was not part of the plan I had for tonight.

He opened his mouth like he wanted to say something but closed it and chewed on his lower lip instead. God. How was it that everything he did was so sexy?

He opened his mouth to try again, but a clatter interrupted him this time. We both turned to look at the kitchen. Lady had knocked off the lid I put over the plate of cheesecake. She pushed her paws into the pie and happily licked the raspberry sauce.

"Lady!" I lunged out of my chair to stop her before she got herself sick. I swear, she made it her mission to do everything she shouldn't. I grabbed Lady before she could ruin the rest of the pie, but I was too late. All that remained of the cheesecake was a mushed mess.

"What the hell, Lady. That was *my* cheesecake." I gave her a soft tap on her forehead, then turned to Caleb.

"I'm sorry, Caleb. It's ruined," I said with genuine disappointment. I was looking forward to eating more of that delicious dessert, and now I couldn't all because of my stupid, but still lovable, cat.

He chuckled at the face I was making. "It's okay. I can always make more. Go ahead and get her cleaned. I'll settle things out here."

He didn't have to help me clean up, but it was sweet of him to offer. "Thanks," I said before heading to the spare bathroom to bathe my naughty cat. Lady hated baths. Well, she was in for a rude awakening, and I had no sympathy for her.

I spent ten minutes wrangling her before I finally got her cleaned. She had drenched me in bath water in her attempts to escape. I wasn't looking too far off from a drowned rat myself.

Caleb entered the bathroom and burst into laughter when he saw my appearance. He grabbed one of the towels I'd placed on the counter for Lady and wrapped it around her before holding her in his hands. "Why don't you get changed? I'll dry the little troublemaker."

"Are you sure? She gets antsy when she's being dried." Lady wasn't a lap cat. She was the kind that only let you hold her for as long as she wanted and not a moment longer.

"Don't worry. Ian's family used to have a cat. He didn't let anyone else but me bathe him. They used to call me the cat whisperer," Caleb joked. He sat on the ground and put Lady on his lap, gently caressing her. Once the shock wore off, she leaned into Caleb's touch and purred.

Well, damn.

Reassured, I left him to his cat whisperer duties while I went to change. Since it was getting late, I didn't bother with a whole new outfit and put on my comfy pajamas instead.

Caleb had cleaned our leftovers and loaded the dishwasher already. He was now sitting on the couch with a soft cat wrapped in a dry towel. She was sleepily snuggled in his arms, and to be honest, I was kinda jealous. Would it be acceptable to toss her from his arms and take her place instead?

He looked up when he heard me. "Hey, I got her mostly dry, but you should keep her somewhere warm just in case." He tried to hand her to me, but she gripped his clothes with her claws and refused to let go.

He gave me a helpless smile, and I chuckled at the scene. Apparently, I wasn't the only one fascinated by this man. "How about we watch the next movie in the series? She'll probably let you go eventually."

And so we did. I got us two glasses of wine and pressed play. We joked throughout the movie and discussed the parts we liked and didn't like.

When the movie ended, Lady had completely fallen asleep on his lap. We looked at each other and shared a secret grin. Caleb gently scooped her from his lap and placed her on the couch. The movement roused her. She blinked awake and jumped off the couch to zoom to my bedroom. Caleb broke out in hysterics, and I joined in with his infectious laughter.

"I've never seen a cat run that fast," he said through gasping breaths. I nodded in agreement, my chuckles too out of control for words.

Our laughs subsided eventually. I looked over at Caleb slouched on the couch, his eyes glazed, and his face flushed from the wine. He was so beautiful. I don't think I'd ever seen anyone more beautiful than him.

He turned to look at me, startled when he found me staring.

"Ahem. It's, um, getting late. I should go." He shifted his eyes away, the tips of his ears burning with shyness. We got off the couch and walked to the door.

"Yeah, you should get some rest. I'll see you in the morning?" I asked while leaning on the doorframe.

He nodded, still looking anywhere but me, and promised, "Tomorrow."

And then he left without turning back. Morning couldn't come soon enough.

THIRTEEN

CALEB

Zack and I went for a morning jog together the next day. This time, I didn't ugly cry on his shirt when we arrived at the lighthouse for a rest. Instead, we laughed and joked about random stupid things. Zack told me stories about the business trips he went on and the chaos he witnessed at some of the restaurants he worked with. I told him about some of the most ridiculous things people have asked if they could deduct from their taxes.

"One guy asked me if he could deduct the cost of building a pool because he planned to have business pool parties. Never mind the fact that he owned a small shop that was online, so he never saw clients in the first place." I did air quotes around the word "business."

Zack chuckled, then sobered. "I guess not all parts of your job are bad, but you still hate it?"

I nodded. He was right. I did encounter some interesting things, and I liked my coworkers well enough, but that wasn't enough to make me like my job. The long hours of poring over boring numbers killed me a little inside.

"Why did you choose the job in the first place?" he asked.

"You're gonna laugh at me if I tell you." I looked at my intertwined fingers.

"I won't. Scout's honor." He brought his hand up to make the gesture.

"Well..." I paused for dramatic effect. "I'm a textbook Virgo, so I searched online for jobs most suited for Virgos, and the results showed accountants as number one. Something about my analytical nature and eye for detail. Plus, accountants make a stable income, so I thought why not?"

Zack didn't say anything. I looked up and saw him biting his fist to hold back his laughter.

"Hey! You promised!" I smacked him on his chest.

He brought his hand up in surrender and said, "Sorry, my bad. I just can't imagine you choosing your career path based on your horoscope. I didn't take you to be the type to believe in that kind of thing."

I lifted my head in a little huff. "Well, they were right about me being good at my job. Numbers made sense to me, but they don't inspire much else. To put it bluntly, it's boring."

Zack cocked his head. He hesitantly asked, "Have you given the bakery more thought?"

"I...I'm thinking about it. I know I would much rather use the money for the CPA on opening my own bakery. However, I have to do my research and be certain that it won't be a complete failure. I need a detailed plan first."

Zack gave me a Cheshire Cat smile. "So, you're saying you would give it serious consideration if you had a detailed plan that showed you wouldn't fail on this endeavor?"

"I...I mean yes, but I would still have to run the numbers and find the funding. Even if I knew the bakery wouldn't fail, it's all pointless if I don't have the capital to actually open the place."

"Yes, of course," he replied. He didn't speak again. We sat

side by side on the bench and watched the waves crash against the shore. I noticed his eyes would occasionally drift to the lighthouse and linger there for a bit. I wondered what he thought when he saw it but didn't have the courage to ask. Instead, we sat in comfortable silence until it was time to head back.

During the jog back to our building, I kept turning over in my head the question Zack had asked me earlier. Had I given the bakery more thought? Of course. It was my dream, but not everyone lived their dreams. If I could be one of the lucky ones who could make their dreams come true, then why shouldn't I take the chance?

Thoughts of a future that I could have bounced around in my mind, and my body was on autopilot as I parted with Zack, showered, and made my trip to the grocery store. It wasn't until I arrived at my mom's place that I snapped back to the present. Conner was sitting on the couch watching a documentary like he always did. He paused the movie and went to grab the rest of the groceries when he saw me. I took the bags I'd carried in and dropped them on the kitchen counter.

"Hi, Mom. I'm here." I gave her a quick peck on her cheek. She glanced at the bags I'd brought in and furrowed her brows. The wrinkles on her forehead became more pronounced than usual.

"Honey, you don't have to bring us groceries every week. We have enough." I knew she felt guilty. Even though I tried to reassure her, she still worried that she was a burden to me.

"It's not out of the way since I do it along with my groceries, so it saves a trip." That was a lie since I got their groceries on my way to their house, but if a little white lie was what it took to make her feel better, then it was worth it. "Besides, can't a son do something nice for his amazing mom?"

Her eyes softened, and I could see the fight leaving her. She wiped her hands on a hand towel and wrapped me up in a hug.

"Thank you, Caleb. You've grown into such a fine man. Your dad would be so proud of you." Little tears pricked my eyes, but I forced them back. I wasn't going to cry over this. If I cried, my mom would start crying with me, and Conner would find us having another cryfest in the kitchen.

Instead, I gave her a tight squeeze before releasing her. "Congratulations on the promotion. It's about time."

A blush suffused her pale cheeks. I'd gotten my dad's hair color but had inherited most of my other features from my mom, including her pale skin and penchant for blushing. It was something Conner teased us about when we both laughed so hard our whole bodies turned red. Conner, on the other hand, had inherited Dad's tan skin and build. He was a nerdy genius, but you couldn't tell just by looking at his physique. He was only sixteen, but already had more muscles than I did.

The way she stood up a little taller told me she was happy about the promotion. "It's nothing. They only gave it to me because the last head waitress left, and I have seniority."

"Hasn't Sally been there longer than you?" I reminded her.

She dismissed my claim. "Sure, but everyone knows she can't be trusted with the position. She's a good waitress, but she always has her head in the clouds. That's the only reason they picked me."

"Mom, stop. You got the job because you deserve it and you're a hard worker. They're lucky to have you." Sometimes, I wanted to shake her until she understood her worth.

She nodded shyly and changed the subject. "Anyway, Conner is leaving for the competition right after his graduation. He'll be gone for a week, so I thought we could go out for Sunday brunch while he's out of town. Maybe get some mimosas."

I took the change in subject for what it was—avoidance. I learned from the best, after all, so I let it slide. "Sounds good."

While we ate, I told them about the possible idea of opening a bakery. It was still far-fetched, but I wanted to get their opinions. Mom was hesitant at first, but she quickly switched to words of encouragement. Conner was on board with it. He loved my desserts and was adamant about receiving free desserts for life at my bakery. I couldn't help bursting out in laughter at his seriousness. I told them not to get their hopes up as I had to come up with the money first, but that didn't stop the gratitude that swelled within me for having a family who loved and supported me.

Monday morning was a drag as always. A pile of paperwork waited on my desk when I arrived at the office. I sighed and prepared myself to meticulously go through all the monotonous papers.

My phone vibrated with a message as I waited for my computer to boot up. I opened it to find a picture of Lady sent by Zack. She was curled up on the couch in the same spot I'd sat in the other night.

Zack: Lady misses you. Come over for dinner tonight? I'm making lasagna.

I smiled when I read the additional text. I noticed that he used the same excuse as last time, but I didn't mind. I needed the excuse just as much as he did.

Caleb: I miss her too. I'll bring dessert.

I tackled my work with renewed energy that I hadn't felt for my job in a long time. The rest of the day went by in a flurry since I was so excited by the thought of seeing Zack again. When the clock hit five, I packed my stuff and speed-walked out of the office. My coworkers shot strange glances at me, but I didn't care. I wanted to get home and bake brownies for Zack tonight.

When the brownies were ready, I packed them and got ready to head over to Zack's. He opened the door as soon as I knocked and flashed me a brilliant smile that stole my breath away. The rest of the night passed in a blur of jokes and us laughing so hard we almost pissed ourselves. Zack had a way of making me laugh like no one else could. When I was with him, I didn't think about the what ifs and just *lived*. This must have been what Ian was talking about.

The following week, Zack and I met up some mornings for a jog. Then, during work, we'd text each other stupid things or share cute cat videos we found online. Close to the end of the day, Zack always found an excuse to invite me over for dinner. He'd tell me he wanted to finish watching the rest of the Thor movies, or he'd request I make a certain dessert for him, or he just didn't want to eat alone. I had no reason to decline since I disliked cooking, and I enjoyed his company. On Thursday, we had dinner together before heading over to Jason and Will's for game night.

On Saturday, Zack invited me to go downtown with him to pick up furniture for the home office he was going to set up in his spare room. He finished his shopping pretty quickly, but we stayed downtown to see the sites and act like tourists in our own city. There were times when I had the strange urge to grab his hand as we strolled through the city, but I had forced those thoughts away as soon as they surfaced.

When dinnertime came around, he dragged me to one of his favorite restaurants near the town's historic clock tower. We lingered at dinner as we discussed our favorite thing about Corio City, the lighthouse for me and the diverse cuisine options for Zack. Hours later, we finally left after our waiter's stares clued us in that we had been occupying the table for far too long.

It wasn't until our morning jog on Sunday that I realized we had spent all our free time this week together. And I was slightly disappointed that I wouldn't be able to have dinner with him tonight since it was Conner's birthday. I could tell Zack was disappointed too since he pouted throughout the whole jog when I told him I was going to my mom's for dinner. His cute expressions just made me want to pinch his cheeks.

Zack sat next to me on our bench by the boardwalk. I enjoyed the stillness of the morning and the comfort of his company. I glanced at him, and my breath caught. I couldn't lie to myself anymore. I was developing feelings for Zack. And I didn't get that antsy feeling I always got whenever emotions were involved. Instead, it felt natural, like Zack was part of the air I breathed. He was just *there*.

Thoughts of Zack swirled through my head on my drive to my mom's. I promised myself I would go with the flow this time and not overthink it, but that didn't stop my traitorous brain. What if things did go further, and we found we weren't compatible as lovers? With that thought in my head, I realized that I couldn't remember what it was like *before*. Before he was there.

Conner grabbed his present and tore it open as soon as I walked through the door. I didn't even have time to shut the door behind me before he let out a high-pitched scream at the sight the digital soldering station he'd been asking for.

"Thank you, thank you, thank you!" he squealed.

"No problem, kid. Happy birthday. You're almost an adult." His happy expression quickly turned to a frown.

"I *am* an adult. Age is just a number," he argued even though we both knew he had one more year before he was legally an adult.

"Okay, whatever you say, kid." I tried to ruffle his hair, but he dodged my hand. He grumbled to himself as he placed his present in the living room before coming back to help me with the grocery bags.

After brunch, Mom and I splayed out on the couch watching a movie. Conner sat on the living room floor experimenting with his new tools. He wanted to adjust a part he was working on for the robotics competition before we went out for dinner tonight.

My phone pinged on the couch beside me, and I opened the message to find a selfie of Zack giving me puppy dog eyes while holding Lady.

Zack: Lady misses you.

I smiled at his message, knowing he was using Lady as an excuse yet again. The man was too adorable.

Caleb: I miss her too.

Zack: Is that all you miss? :)

Caleb: I miss your parmesan chicken too. Man, that was good.

He sent back a crying emoji that brought a laugh out of me.

"Who's making you laugh like that?" My mom's voice brought me out of the trance I got caught up in every time I talked with Zack. He had a way of making me forget about everything around me.

"Uh, no one. Just a friend." I glanced at the message Zack sent back. He said he'd make the chicken for me tomorrow night for dinner. Another smile spread on my face at how easily he brought up us eating together like it was a normal thing.

Mom leaned in toward me to try and peek at my phone. I turned off the screen and placed it face down on the couch.

"Mom, what are you doing?" I gave her a gentle push. I didn't want her to see the picture Zack had sent me. She'd have questions if she saw, and I didn't know if I had the answers.

"Oh, nothing. I just wanted to see who was making my son so happy. I wouldn't have to snoop if my son just told me." She crossed her arms, giving me a half-serious stern look.

"It's nobody. Just my neighbor. He sent me a picture of his cat." I shrugged, trying to act casual.

"The new one? Your *hot* new neighbor?" Mom perked up at the hint of gossip.

"*Mom.* Please don't say that. You're my mom. You're not supposed to find anyone hot." I mentally gagged at the thought of my mom thinking Zack was hot. He was, but that didn't mean I wanted my mom to think that.

"Hey! Just because I'm old doesn't mean I'm dead. I still find people hot. Why, we have several regulars at the diner who are very handsome," she huffed.

I leaned toward her with interest. Mom never mentioned guys. All the times I'd nagged her about finding a partner fell on deaf ears. Sometimes it surprised me how similar we were. She'd lecture me about finding love and companionship, yet avoided the topic when the tables were turned. Perhaps she was finally taking her own advice and had taken an interest in someone.

"So...Have you taken a liking to any of those handsome regulars?" I asked cautiously. Mom averted her eyes, and a blush crept up her cheeks.

"You have, haven't you? Who is it? How long have you guys been going out?" I pointed at her and gasped. Conner looked up from his place on the floor, also taking an interest in the topic.

Mom glanced between the two of us before settling her gaze on me and sputtered, "I...We're not...I mean..."

"Oh, my god. Mom, you have a crush on someone! You have to tell us everything!" Conner leaped from the floor and sat on the other side of Mom.

"A crush?" she asked incredulously, although her red cheeks gave her away. "It's nothing like that. It's just one of the regulars. We talk when the diner isn't busy. He considers me a friend."

"Uh-huh. And how often does this *friend* of yours eat at the diner?" I asked. I suspected there was more to it than my mom was letting on, and I was ready to get to the bottom of it.

"Uh, well...I mean, he's not a very good cook, and he likes the food at the diner. Plus, we have that new healthy menu now, so—"

"How often, Mom?" I interrupted her rambling. That was something else that I'd inherited from her.

"He eats most meals at the diner. But that's only because it's close to his office, and we offer healthy meals," she quickly added.

"No matter how healthy the meals are, you'll get sick of eating the same thing all the time eventually. He's obviously there to see you, Mom," Conner chimed in.

"Did he ask you out yet?" I almost bounced out of my seat with excitement.

Mom tucked a piece of hair behind her ear. She only did that when she was too embarrassed by what she had to say next. I smelled juicy gossip.

"Well...We both have an interest in the historical landmarks in Corio City. He said the clock tower has guided tours and asked if I wanted to go with him." Mom wasn't looking either of us in the eye. Instead, she was staring intently at the vase that sat in the corner of the room.

"Mom!" I shouted. "You have to go. When is it? You're going on this date." Conner nodded in agreement.

"It...It's not a date," she protested. "I'm sure he just wants some companionship. Finding friends at our age isn't easy, you know."

"Whatever." Conner rolled his eyes at her. "You can call it whatever you want, but you have to go. Mom, I'm off to college this fall, and I worry at the thought of you being here all alone. I know you never dated because of me and Caleb, but we're grown now. We can take care of ourselves. It's time for you to take care of yourself."

A stray tear slid down her cheek, and she swiped it with her finger. "When did you become so mature?" She reached out and ruffled Conner's hair.

"Mom!" he called out, moving his head out of her grasp. He hated when anyone messed with his hair.

"So...you'll go out with him?" I pushed. I wanted so much for her to be happy and although she claimed to be happy with just Conner and me, we couldn't be her whole life. It was time she showed the world what a beautiful and amazing woman she was and found someone deserving of her love.

She opened her mouth before closing it again. "Maybe," she finally said.

We grinned wide smiles at her. She didn't say no. It was a start.

FOURTEEN

ZACK

Caleb and I spent practically every free moment of the week together. Being around him felt like being enveloped in warmth, and it calmed something in me. I imagined us as a family when we sat down together for dinner. We'd talk about our day, even if nothing interesting had happened, and make each other laugh. It was warm and perfect. And I never wanted it to end.

It became glaringly obvious on Sunday how much his presence calmed me. Caleb had already left for his mom's, and Lady and I were lounging on the couch watching whatever came on the TV. It was the same thing we always did, but it felt wrong today. *Because Caleb wasn't here.* And there was that tiny voice prickling in the back of my head again.

I turned off the TV and stood to stretch. If I stayed in my apartment, I'd end up thinking about Caleb all day. I needed to do something more productive instead. I'd been doing research about the bakeries in the area all week and planned to visit Osona's bakery today. I'd been meaning to visit her since Caleb told me they were shutting down, but so far, I hadn't gotten the chance to. Now was the perfect time.

Osona was one of my first clients in Corio City. She and her husband had opened their bakery almost fifty years ago. They were one of the pillars of Corio City back when it was just a small town. However, when the world entered a new age and the era of fast food came, they couldn't keep up. Their business slowly dwindled as people turned to more modern and cheap establishments. However, they didn't give up. The bakery had been their dream for half their lives, and they'd refused to let it die. They wanted to leave a legacy for their children. That was why they had consulted with my company.

I was put in charge of the project and helped them rebrand. I set up social media accounts for their business and made all of Corio City aware of their presence. They implemented all the changes I'd suggested and worked hard to make their business thrive again. That was why I was shocked when Caleb told me they were closing down. From what they'd told me before, they were going to have one of their children inherit the business. That was what I wanted to find out today.

Seeing the bakery again reminded me how much I loved working with businesses that I was able to keep a long-term relationship with. Since the bakery was located in Corio City, I'd been able to keep in touch with Osona and watch as she made the business into what it was today. I was starting to realize that I was tired of traveling and taking on short-term jobs that I eventually had to leave behind. I wanted to help businesses in Corio City, where I could watch them grow even after our contracts were over.

My desire to stay in Corio City wasn't the only reason behind my thoughts. Things had been a little tense and a whole lot awkward at work these past couple of weeks. Joshua avoided ever being alone with me and did his best to not have to speak to me at all. He was never rude, nor did he ever purposefully alienate me. He just acted almost...scared of me.

I confronted him about it one day, and he looked terrified like I was going to call the cops on him or something. He gave me the "it's not you, it's me," line and apologized, and since then, he made more of an effort to not avoid me. It was very apparent that he was haunted by ghosts from his past, but that wasn't my business. As long as we could maintain a polite work relationship, that was all that mattered.

Thankfully, my projects that were set to finish in the fall were all in Corio City, and I didn't have to travel for them. As crazy as it was, I loathed the idea of being away from Caleb.

Summer was usually a slow period for the company, so I wasn't worried about receiving new projects for now. And if I did, I could ask Scott if he'd be willing to take them. I played with the idea of letting the company know I was quitting once my current projects finished, and it was quite tempting.

I had enough savings to last me a while if I didn't find a new job right away. The only question was, what would I do with myself? I could start my own small firm that only catered to the businesses here in the city. I imagined working at the bakery with Caleb. We would work side by side to make the place flourish like Osona and her husband had. We'd do it together.

I shook my head at that thought. We were nothing like Osona and her husband. We weren't together, for one, and Caleb was still on the fence about going through with his dream. That was the whole reason I was visiting Osona today— to formulate a plan to convince Caleb that it didn't just have to be a dream. He could make it a reality.

Business was flowing steadily inside the bakery. A young woman I'd never seen before was manning the front. She was probably a part-timer. Osona came out carrying a tray of freshly baked bread. She was in her seventies, but you couldn't tell by her appearance. Lugging all the bread around every day had kept her in shape.

"Osona." I waved to get her attention. She glanced up from what she was doing, and a smile lit up her face when she caught sight of me.

"Why, is that you, Zack? My goodness! It's been ages. How are you, dear?" Osona surrounded me with one of her mama bear hugs before pulling away. She grabbed my hand and dragged me to the back where they had a tiny sitting area the staff used for breaks.

"I'm doing good. Work has calmed down a bit, so I haven't been traveling as much. How have you been?" I took the cup of tea she offered and sat on the tiny sofa crammed in the corner of the room.

"Same ol', same ol'. Another day, another bread. You know how it is." She gave me a wink. "So, what brings you by today? You're a rare visitor."

I rubbed the back of my head, embarrassed. I should have come to visit more often since we'd developed a friendship in the time we worked together. Once they discovered that I spent most holidays alone, they were kind enough to invite me to their house to spend the holidays with them. It was no excuse, but work and life had gotten so busy that I hadn't had time to come by. I would visit them more often in the future, be it at their bakery or their house.

"I heard you were closing the bakery. What happened? I thought one of your kids was going to inherit it?"

Osona sighed in response. She took a sip of her own tea before putting it down and speaking. "Those brats. They all said they didn't want the pressure of owning a business. I guess they saw how much we struggled in those years and got frightened. They have their own lives now, and they're happy. And now that we're getting older, we can't run this place for much longer, so what else can we do?"

"Well..." I started. "What do you think about selling the place?"

She raised her brow at me. "Do you know someone that's interested? You know that I wouldn't sell my baby to some incompetent fool just to have them ruin the business. Even if the name of the bakery changes, it will always be my baby."

I nodded in understanding. Even if the whole business changed, who would want to see the place they poured their life and blood into fall into ruin? "Don't worry. His desserts can rival yours. He makes the most amazing cookies that I think are his own inventions. They just melt right in your mouth."

Osona gave me another eyebrow raise, then smirked. "You clearly like more than just his desserts. Tell me, who is this young man that makes you talk so animatedly?"

I glanced away from her, feeling shy talking about my crush. "He...he's my neighbor. But I wouldn't praise his baking if I didn't think it was good. I wouldn't betray my work ethic like that. He's the real deal."

"I see." She crossed her arms and placed a finger underneath her chin. "If that's the case, I'd like to test him. If he pleases me, I'll sell the place to him."

"There's just one thing. He doesn't have a lot of capital for a venture. I'm looking into grants and loans for him, but that's one of the main reasons he hasn't opened his own bakery yet." Logically speaking, Osona had every right to reject the deal just based on that. No businessperson would want to make a losing deal. I wouldn't blame her if she refused.

Osona placed a hand on top of mine. "Oh, honey. You know we started out with nothing as well. If he's as good as you say he is, then I'm sure we can work something out. Places have souls, you know?" She glanced out into the commercial kitchen where her husband was busy baking. Her eyes saw more than just what was there. "We put so much love and energy into this place. All the memories we've made here have manifested into something more than just a store. Shutting it down forever is our last option. All we want is for this bakery to have someone who will love the place and treat it with respect like we have."

I nodded even though I didn't really understand. I had never treasured a place before. I lived like a ghost in my childhood house. There was no comfort or love. No memories to make the place a home.

I thought back to the week I spent with Caleb. Caleb sitting on my couch, showing me something stupid on TV. The night he tried to help me cook, and I discovered that even though he was an amazing baker, he was a hopeless chef. We were watching a movie one night after dinner when Caleb had fallen asleep, and his head had landed on my shoulder. I'd wrapped my arm around him to steady him. His soft breaths tickled my skin, and underneath the heat of arousal that burned in me, there was a sense of rightness. Maybe I did understand what she meant.

Osona and I chatted for a bit longer before I left. I gave her and her husband a hug and promised to visit more often. I told her I'd call her to arrange a date to bring Caleb over for the test, if he agreed. Since she said there was no rush, I wanted to do a little bit more research, but I hoped to tell him the news within the month.

It was lunchtime when I left. Not wanting to cook for one, I picked up some takeout and brought it home to eat. Lady greeted me at the door, then sauntered to the couch for an afternoon nap. I also brought my food to the couch and sat in my normal spot. I glanced to my right where Caleb usually sat when he was over, and a sudden unease shot through me. I was being stupid. We'd only been hanging out for a week, and I already considered having Caleb by my side as the new normal. That was a whole can of worms I wasn't ready to open, so I took a selfie with Lady instead and sent it to him.

We texted for a bit before he stopped replying. He told me today was his younger brother's birthday, so I figured he was off spending time with his family. Setting my phone down, I leaned my head against the back of my couch. *What the heck was I supposed to do with myself now?*

The next couple of weeks went by in honeymoon-like bliss, and I had to constantly remind myself that Caleb and I weren't together. Sure, we had dinner together almost every night and texted throughout the day, but that didn't mean anything. Right? At this point, I didn't know anymore. My brain had trouble differentiating between what was allowed as friends versus what was allowed as lovers.

Caleb had defaulted to baking at my place since I had a larger kitchen, and he claimed my cabinets weren't as low-hanging as his. It worked for me since it meant I had first dibs on whatever sweets he made. I'd found out that Saturday was the day he baked extra desserts for his friends.

I stood on the other side of the kitchen counter watching Caleb sway his hips to the radio. The little jiggle of his butt hypnotized me, and I made my way behind him in a trance. My hand reached out to bring him in my arms when he turned around and jumped in surprise to find me right behind him.

"What are you doing?" he asked, a little more skittish than usual.

"I, uh...I just wanted to grab a glass. I'm thirsty." I paused to process what just came out of my mouth. "For water. I didn't mean anything else. Just wanted to grab some water."

He chuckled and turned around to grab a glass from the cabinet. "Here. Have at it, big guy. We can't have you shriveling up now, can we?"

He felt comfortable teasing me now, but when we had actual physical contact, he would get all shy again. When I grabbed the glass from him and our fingers accidentally touched, his breath hitched, and he glanced away. He didn't move his hand immediately. The seconds stretched out until it became almost awkward for us to stand there and hold hands, and he finally let go and turned back to his prepping.

"So...what are you making?" I filled my glass with water and sipped on it as I leaned against the counter to watch him work.

"Oh, a cake." He kept his back to me and continued slicing strawberries.

"I love cake. What kind?" I reached to grab a piece of the red fruit, but he slapped my hand away.

"Sorry, sweet tooth. The cake isn't for you."

"It's not?" My voice squeaked in a way that was unnatural to my deep timbre.

"No, it's for Noah." Caleb turned around and laughed at the pout that was pasted on my face.

"Noah?" The squeak persisted. I didn't like the fact that he was making desserts for another man. Sure, he made desserts for his friends, but he never made a whole damn cake for them before.

"Yeah, our neighbor, Noah." He tilted his head, presumably confused at my own confusion. I didn't know we had a neighbor named Noah. We had four units on this floor, and I still hadn't met the person who lived in the unit across from mine. That must have been the mysterious Noah. However, that didn't answer the question of why he was baking a whole freaking cake for him.

"So...um, why are you baking a cake for him?" I tried to keep the jealousy out of my voice, but I doubted I succeeded, which was made evident by Caleb's laugh ringing through the kitchen.

"It's for his birthday, silly. Noah rarely leaves his apartment. He's not a people person, but he's a nice guy. I thought I'd make him a cake so that he'd have something sweet today." He put the finished strawberries to the side and poured ingredients into a large bowl. "Don't worry. I didn't forget about you. I have extra macadamia nuts. How do you feel about nut cookies?" he asked with a gleam in his eye.

I cringed, recalling our disastrous first meeting. Heck if I knew why he agreed to dinner with me after our initial meeting, which included many mentions of nuts. Mainly mine. Caleb laughed when he saw my expression, one of his cute snorts coming through in his excitement.

"Or maybe not. I'll make you chocolate brownies later," he said, much to my relief.

"Yessss! I love chocolate!" I shouted with my hands above my head. Caleb chuckled and returned to what he'd been doing. I let him be and waited patiently on the couch with Lady for my sweets. I could forgive Noah for stealing Caleb's cake. Just for today.

FIFTEEN

CALEB

More weeks passed, and we settled into a routine that should have scared me but didn't. Zack stopped asking me to eat dinner with him. Instead, there was a silent acknowledgement that eating dinner together was just what we did.

I came home Friday evening feeling exhausted from a busy day at work. Zack said he wanted to try a new recipe tonight, and I was looking forward to it. However, I knew I couldn't stay awake until dinner was ready. I dropped my briefcase as soon as I entered my home and loosened my tie. I didn't bother changing into my pajamas before taking off my glasses and flopping on my bed and passing out. I figured I'd take a quick power nap before dinner.

The sound of knocking woke me. I rubbed my sleepy eyes awake and was startled to find the world around me shrouded in darkness. I woke up my phone and checked the time. *Shit!* Zack had sent me some text messages asking me where I was. I thrust my glasses on and leaped out of bed and ran to the door. He probably came to check up since I never replied to his messages.

When I opened the door, Zack was there. He looked relieved to see me. When he had a good look at me, he chuckled and reached out to me. "Your glasses are crooked, sleepyhead." He straightened them, then proceeded to run his fingers through my wavy hair to fix the monster of a bedhead I probably had.

"Hi." My voice cracked, still stiff from my slumber. I tried again. "Hi. Sorry, I was gonna take a quick nap, but I guess I overslept. Did you eat yet?" He shook his head. "Oh my god, I'm so sorry. Are you hungry? That's a stupid question. Of course you're hungry. It's hours past our usual dinnertime. You should've eaten without me. I'm sorry." The more I spoke, the more I worked myself up. The guilt at making him wait ate at me, and I lowered my head in shame.

He used his finger to lift my chin so that I wasn't staring at the ground anymore. "Hey, no need to be sorry. I would gladly starve if it meant getting to eat with you. I know you're tired, but you should eat something before going to sleep, sweets."

A million bees buzzed in my stomach. He'd started calling me that nickname last week because he said I was like his personal sweets factory. He also told me the nickname fit me since I was as sweet as the desserts I made. I was pretty sure he said the last part to get a rise out of me. He loved teasing me 'til I blushed. And knowing that fact made me redden quicker because deep down I knew I enjoyed the teasing as well.

"Go change into something more comfortable. I'll heat up our food." He pulled my necktie completely off. He then used his other hand to grab my limp hand and placed the tie in it, his fingers lingered for a couple seconds longer than what was socially acceptable for just friends.

Then there was that. In the last week, Zack had taken to finding reasons to casually touch me. Our fingers would brush when we handed each other things, or his leg would press against mine when we were watching movies on the couch. It was never direct. It almost seemed like he was afraid of scaring me off, so he made his touches casual. He was right, of course. I probably would have sprinted out of the room if he made a sudden move. His casual brushes allowed me to get used to his touch, making me crave them even more.

I stood dazed by the open door long after he left. The heat he left still lingered, and I stared at my hand like it wasn't a part of me. I was tingly and light, and I knew from the bottom of my heart that I was falling. Hard. I wanted more than just these light touches. I wanted his magical hands all over my body, but I didn't want him to be just a hookup. Because he wasn't. He was so much more than that. He brought out feelings in me that I'd never tested before and...I didn't know what to do with that.

The sound of the door opening broke me from my trance.

"Caleb?" Zack's shout sounded from the hallway. I could imagine him sticking his head out the door in search of me.

"Coming," I called back. I almost stumbled in my haste to get to my room but caught myself before I tripped and fell flat on my face. I didn't need to show up to dinner with a red mark on my forehead. I was already embarrassed enough.

I scrambled to change into my pajamas and checked in the mirror to make sure I looked somewhat presentable. When I arrived at Zack's apartment, he was sitting at the set table waiting for me. His bright smile gave me that loopy feeling again. The drowsiness from earlier was completely gone as I settled in the seat across from him. We talked about our day during dinner, and afterwards, we stood side by side while I washed the dishes and he dried them.

"Do you want to watch a movie?" he asked after the cleanup. We both knew that I would probably fall asleep during the movie since I was still tired, and movies made me even more sleepy, but I said yes anyway. Every time I fell asleep on the couch, I woke up cradled in his arms. And that was exactly where I wanted to be right now. I didn't make it past the twenty-minute mark. My head landed on a solid shoulder as I drifted to dreamland with Richard Gere's voice in the background. In my half-asleep state, I swore I felt someone giving my forehead a soft kiss. Or maybe I was dreaming, but what a beautiful dream it was.

When I opened my eyes again, the TV was off, and I was lying on top of warm muscles. My glasses had been removed. I looked down to see Zack asleep under me. He had his arms around me, and his hands rested on my lower back. A purring lump curled on my upper back completed our dog-pile—or should I say cat-pile. Lady laid on top of us, claiming the status of queen of this apartment. She naturally was, of course.

I struggled to get up so I wasn't crushing Zack, but his arms tightened around me, and I fell back flush against him.

"Shh. You'll wake Lady," he mumbled sleepily. He brought one hand up to my head and gently pushed it so my ear was in line with his chest. The soft stroking of my hair, his strong heartbeat against my ear, and Lady's purrs eventually lulled me back to sleep.

If this was a dream, I never wanted it to end.

It wasn't a dream, unfortunately. A loud crash woke me up the next day. The loud crash was...me falling off the couch and landing on the carpet.

"Oww," I groaned as I used a hand to rub out the kink in my neck I had developed from sleeping in a weird position all night. Zack lifted his head from the couch and looked at me in a daze.

"Wha...What's going on? Are you okay?" He rubbed the sleepiness from his eyes when he saw me sprawled on the ground. He tried to get off the couch but winced.

"Damn, I'm all stiff." He stretched his arms above his head, cracking his back in the process. "I guess that's what we get for falling asleep on the couch." He smirked at me.

I looked away, embarrassed by the fact that we slept all night in each other's arms. I stood up, my back turned to him so that he couldn't see my blush, and I walked to the door.

"I should get going," I told him, still not daring to look him in the eye.

Zack grabbed my hand before I could get far. "Hey, you all right?" His voice sounded concerned.

I nodded, not trusting my mouth. I would be a rambling mess if I said anything now.

"Do you want to go for a walk? I'm sure it'll help loosen our muscles." He still hadn't let go. Instead, he used his thumb to rub tiny circles on the back of my hand.

I nodded again before breaking his hold and running out of there like my ass was on fire. I needed to calm the fuck down. I wasn't a blushing virgin, but I was acting like one. I blamed it all on Zack. His presence did something to my body. To me.

When I cooled down enough to think clearly, I washed up and put on my contacts. My glasses were still at Zack's, and I made a mental note to get them from him later. I changed into my workout clothes and got ready to meet him.

Zack brought Lady on the walk with us. I laughed when I saw the very bedazzled pink leash he took out.

"What?" he asked. "Lady deserves a leash fitting a queen." I couldn't argue with that.

The walk was exactly what I needed. Zack didn't push me to talk about last night. His silent presence allowed me to organize my thoughts and made me realize that Zack no longer belonged in any box I had. He'd crawled his way out of the friends box and marathoned toward the one closest to my heart. I wanted him. I knew that now, and the truth felt like it burned deep in my bones. The question was—how was I supposed to get him? I'd never been in a relationship before. I didn't even know what relationships were supposed to be like. I'd spent my whole life taking care of my family and pursuing my career. Getting involved with someone used to be the furthest thing from my mind, but now all that had changed.

We didn't walk to the lighthouse since we had Lady with us, but we found benches close to our building to sit and enjoy the morning sun. Zack kept Lady's leash on her, but didn't keep a hold of it and let her wander around the area.

"Aren't you afraid she'll run away?" I asked as I nervously watched Lady sniff the flower growing on the side of the board-walk. She might not have been my cat, but I had formed an emotional connection to her.

"Nah, she never goes far, and she knows when to come back." Zack stretched his head back, the soft morning sun casting a warm glow on his tan skin. I compelled my eyes to stop staring and went back to watching Lady. Another cat had appeared, and it was cautiously approaching Lady.

I tugged at Zack's sleeve and pointed to the unknown cat, worried that they would start fighting. I read somewhere that cats were very territorial.

"Don't worry. Lady is usually good with other cats. Plus, it's good for Lady to make other feline friends." Zack must have said that to reassure me since he stood up and slowly crept closer to the two cats. He had his hand out like he was ready to intervene if this broke out in a cat fight. The two cats circled before sniffing each other and laying down to continue basking in the sun. Thankfully, no claws were coming out this morning.

We went back to our respective apartments after the walk. I lay on my couch, freshly showered and thinking about what to do for lunch, as breakfast time had come and gone a long time ago. I reached for my phone to find a restaurant to get delivery when Zack texted me.

Zack: What do you want for lunch?

Well, I guess that settled it. I wasn't about to say no to a gorgeous man who wanted to cook for me. It was a plus that he was an amazing chef. I loved baking, but not cooking. It had always stressed me out for reasons I couldn't figure out. Maybe it was the fact that food recipes didn't have concrete measurements—how much was a dash anyway? Or perhaps it was because cooking was done at a much faster pace than baking. Whatever the reason was, it meant that my cooking skills were severely lacking, but that didn't mean I couldn't help prep.

Caleb: Anything. I could eat a horse right now. I'll help.

We sprawled out on the couch after the delicious meal. Zack played on his phone while I stared at the TV without actually watching it.

Zack made no indications of wanting to kick me out, and I sure as heck wasn't leaving of my own accord. I wanted his calm presence as I figured out how to broach the topic of being *more*. A shot of worry filled me with thoughts of his rejection. What if he didn't want to be anything more? What if he did, but later, we broke up? I was pretty certain that he wasn't an international spy, but that didn't mean he didn't have secrets. He could be, I don't know, a werewolf or something. If he was, he was one sexy werewolf. I'd let him mount me any day.

"Caleb," Zack's voice cut through my mental fog. "What are you thinking about?" His signature smirk appeared on his face.

"N-nothing! I wasn't thinking about anything. Especially not about werewolves or mounting. Nope, not at all." I put a hand over my mouth to shut myself up before I said more stupid things.

He raised an eyebrow in amusement. "Okayyy. Did you hear my question?"

"What question?" I asked. Obviously, I was too busy imagining sexy time with a certain werewolf to hear any questions from the mortal world.

"Eric asked if we wanna go to Joe's tonight. He said Ian's bringing his friends. I assume he means Jason and Will."

"How does Ian know Eric?" I asked skeptically. I hoped they hadn't hooked up. It would be all I'd think about if we were in a group together.

"They bonded over the full moon crazies." I raised my eyebrow in question, and he chuckled. "Don't ask. Anyway, pub tonight?"

I hated places that specialized in serving drinks. They were loud and crowded and chaotic. To someone who liked order and tranquility, it was basically my worst nightmare come true.

"I don't know..." I began. My phone beeped with a new text message. I took a glance and saw it was from Ian.

Ian: You're coming out tonight. Don't even think about bailing. I miss hanging out with my best friend.

I swear, he could read my mind. If not, how did he send a message right when I was about to reject the offer?

"I guess I'm going." I showed Zack the text from Ian.

After dinner—Zack cooked, of course—the five of us piled into Ian's minivan and headed to the pub. Eric and Scott, Zack's coworker, were already waiting for us at the pub. It was crowded since it was a Saturday night, and Joe's was the gay pub to go to for weekend hookups. Or at least that was what Ian had told me.

They were waiting in an empty circle booth that looked big enough to fit all of us. A pitcher of beer and glasses were already scattered on the table.

"My man, you're alive! How's the honeymoon period?"

Eric got up to give Zack a one-armed hug. Zack pushed him away with a glare.

"Shut up," he gritted out and shot a nervous glance my way. Why were they talking about a honeymoon? To my knowledge, Zack wasn't dating anyone. He spent practically all his time with me. There was no way he had time for someone else, right?

We all settled into the booth and gave a round of introductions before breaking off into small talk. Jason sat at one end with Will right beside him. A stranger came up to our table and said something to Jason. A heavy scowl formed on Will's face. He put his arm around Jason and said something to scare the stranger away. Will nudged Jason out of the seat and had him sit on the inside while Will sat at the edge. He put his arms around Jason, looking unhappy, and Jason gave him a goofy smile, and his head tilted in confusion.

My eyes widened, and I turned to Ian, who sat next to me. "Are they..." I covered my mouth to block them from seeing.

Ian rolled his eyes at me. "Took you long enough to figure it out, you blockhead. I swear, you're so dense sometimes."

I gaped at him. I met Will and Jason four years ago when I had moved into the building. We hung out almost every week for game night, and I didn't sense a thing. "So...they're dating?" I asked skeptically. Sure, Will acted weird around Jason sometimes, but I never saw them acting romantic with each other. I thought they were like Ian and me, but obviously not if they were doing the dirty together.

Ian shook his head. "Will is...working on it."

Ah. Unrequited love. I could relate. After realizing that Zack refused to stay in the nice and orderly box I placed him in, it felt like my body was at war with itself. I wanted the comfort he gave me by being by my side, but I also wanted to run and hide so that I didn't have mini-Caleb constantly telling me all the things that could go wrong.

What if he rejected me, and our friendship was ruined? What if he agreed, then we broke up, and our friendship was ruined? The only outcome my brain could envision happening was the end of our friendship, and I didn't know if that was something I could accept.

Ian put his arms around me and pulled me closer. "Tell me everything."

"W-what do you mean? What's there to tell?"

He narrowed his eyes and said, "Cut the bullshit. What's going on between you and Zack?"

"Shh!" I turned to look at my other side where Zack sat. Thankfully, he was engrossed in a story Eric was telling dramatically with wild hand gestures. "He's gonna hear."

"Then let's go somewhere else. We'll sit by the bar."

I got up to follow Ian out of the booth. Zack grabbed my hand when he saw me getting up. "Where are you going?"

"Ian and I are going to the bar," I replied. My eyes were locked at the spot where our hands touched. Would it be weird if I weaved my fingers through his? He followed my gaze to our hands and released his hold on me, much to my dismay.

"I'll go with you guys. We need another round anyway."

I turned back to give Ian a shrug. He rolled his eyes at me again.

It was crowded by the bar, but we managed to squeeze through a gap to get to the front. Zack waved his hand, and a cute and petite redhead came up to serve us.

"Well, well. If it isn't Zack. It's been a while, darling. What can I getcha?" The redhead gave Zack a wink. My eyes widened, and I turned to Ian for guidance. *Was he flirting with Zack?* I tried to ask with my eyes. Ian just looked at me and shrugged, providing no assistance at all.

"Hey, Alfie. Can we get a couple of pitchers? Maybe some peanuts," Zack replied. He was standoffish and didn't respond to the redhead's—Alfie's—chummy behavior.

"Anything for you, Zack. *Anything*." Alfie ran a finger up Zack's arm, giving him another flirtatious wink. Okay, he was definitely flirting. I saw red, and it wasn't Alfie's red hair I was seeing. I'd never been jealous over a guy before, but I now knew it was red. Blind fury clouded my vision, and I'd be damned if I didn't show everyone at the bar that Zack was mine. Well, he didn't belong to me, at least not yet, but he was... my Zack.

I stepped up to the bar and pressed myself against Zack's side. I hooked my arm through his and gave him my most inno-cent nothing-out-of-the-ordinary look. "Zack, who's this?"

Zack looked at me with wide eyes before his confused expression morphed into a wide grin. He unhooked his arm and brought it around me instead, pushing us even closer together. "Sweets, this is Alfie. He works at the pub. Alfie, this is Caleb. He's my..." He looked at me for help.

"Boyfriend," I blurted. "I'm his boyfriend." I leaned my head against Zack's shoulder to stake my claim on the man. I wanted to make it absolutely clear that this feisty twink had no place flirting with Zack. Zack vibrated against me. I glanced at him and saw that he was holding back a laugh. This was no laughing matter, and I pushed my elbow into his gut to make sure he knew it.

"Ahem. Yes, Caleb is my beautiful and amazing boyfriend." Hints of amusement laced his voice. I elbowed him again to get him to cut it out. It didn't work. "Caleb, my one and only schnookums, how was I lucky enough to land someone like you? Really, *please* tell me."

I shrugged off his arm and huffed, my face already burning from embarrassment. Thankfully, the pub was dark enough that you wouldn't be able to tell unless you stuck your face right in front of mine.

"Oh, honey. Don't get mad. You know I can't stand it when my cupcake is angry with me." Zack continued his teasing.

I ignored him and turned to Alfie. "Give me your strongest shot. Give me whatever that'll let me forget the last ten minutes."

Alfie took down our order and sighed. "All the good ones are taken," he muttered under his breath.

Zack chuckled and wrapped his arm around me again. "Muffin, don't be angry at me. Your *boyfriend* will get sad."

I covered my face with my hands and groaned. I created a monster.

SIXTEEN

ZACK

I was surprised when Caleb called me his boyfriend. Surprised, but pleased. It showed that he was also affected by...whatever this was between us. He was so adorable when he acted jealous and tried to claim me in front of Alfie. If only he knew. I didn't have eyes for anyone else but him. He was all I could see.

We hung out and joked with the boys for the rest of the night. We took turns at the pool table, and I found that Caleb and his friends were pretty competitive.

"My grandma has better aim than you," Ian taunted Scott, who was aiming for the striped number two.

Caleb, who was to be on Scott's team, shot up in his defense. "Oh, yeah? Well, my...my grandma handles balls better than you can!"

Scott missed his shot and turned to face Caleb. "Dude, what?"

Caleb rubbed the back of his neck. "You know, balls." He pointed at the balls on the pool table, and we all burst out in laughter. He was too cute for words.

They finished the game, and Eric bought us all a round of

shots. Caleb was starting to get tipsy thanks to the shot he already had at the bar.

"God, he's such a lightweight." Ian nudged Caleb off his shoulder and pushed him against me. I caught him as he looped his arms around my neck and snuggled close. I didn't mind one bit. If tipsy Caleb meant I got to hold him in my arms, I was all for it. Caleb took a sniff before snuggling closer to me. My heart melted.

We stayed another hour before calling it a night. Caleb had fallen asleep on the table, and I kept watch next to him.

"Sweets, get up. It's time to go home," I whispered in his ear. He mumbled something in his sleep and turned his face away from me. I gave his shoulder another shake. "Caleb." My calls were futile as his eyes remained firmly shut.

Ian stood next to me and poked Caleb's cheek. "He's passed out cold," he commented. "Should I get Will to carry him?" The others were waiting outside for us. We were supposed to meet them after waking Caleb up, but he refused to come back to the world of the living.

"Nah, I'll carry him," I said. I wasn't going to let Caleb snuggle in another man's arms. "Caleb," I tried again, lifting him from the table. He turned toward me this time and hooked his arms around my neck. I pulled him off the booth and wrapped his legs around me. He hung off of me like a koala, and I placed my hands under his plump butt to keep him in place.

I was thankful I spent all those hours lifting weights in the gym with Eric. Caleb wasn't extremely heavy, but his taller frame made things a bit awkward and put a strain on muscles I hadn't used in a long time. I managed to get him in the car without incident. Ian drove us back home while Caleb was tucked in my arms, where he belonged.

When we arrived at our building, Caleb woke up just

enough to walk on his own while leaning heavily against me. We said goodnight to Ian on the first floor; then the four of us took the elevator to the second floor. Sure, we could've taken the stairs, but we were all too tired for that shit.

"Do you need help?" Will's deep voice asked when we arrived on our floor. Jason opened the door to their apartment and stumbled inside. He was falling asleep on his feet as well.

"I got him. You go take care of your man." I shot him a knowing look, and he returned an acknowledging glance before leaving Caleb and me alone in the hallway.

"Sweets, we're here. You have to unlock your door." I gently shook him again, but he refused to open his eyes.

"No. Wanna stay with you," he muttered against my skin, his warm breath making my skin tingle. I wasn't going to argue with that. I very much liked the idea of holding Caleb while we slept.

I managed to unlock and open my door with Caleb hanging off me. Lady greeted us by the door like she always did, and she let out an annoyed meow, probably peeved that we came home so late. I laid Caleb on my bed and took off his shoes before entering my ensuite bathroom to grab an extra toothbrush and towel in case he wanted to wash up before he slept.

I reentered my bedroom and shook Caleb again. "Sweets, at least take out your contacts before you sleep. They'll irritate your eyes if you sleep with them in. I also got you a toothbrush."

He must not have liked the idea of sleeping with contacts in either since he groggily stood up, and I helped him into the bathroom. He washed his hands and quickly took out his contacts. I stayed in the bathroom and watched him to make sure he didn't poke his eyes out. After the contacts were out and thrown away, he stumbled back into my room, presumably to pass out again.

I quickly washed up and changed into my pajamas. I found

Caleb sprawled on top of the sheets in only his underwear. He had on black briefs that outlined the curves of his ass in a perfect way. I forced myself to look away from his assets before I did something I'd regret. I maneuvered him under the covers and slid in beside him. When I settled down, Caleb turned to face me and shuffled close. I wrapped my arms around him and listened to his soft breaths against my skin as I fell asleep.

The morning light shining on my face woke me up. Caleb had turned over sometime in his sleep, and I was now spooning him from behind, his ass cradled against my morning wood. I could tell he was awake by his breathing. He was stiff, and I could almost hear the gears turning a million miles an hour in his head.

"Stop thinking." My voice rasped, still languid with sleep. He flinched at the sound of my voice and leaped from my arms.

"I...I didn't mean to wake you. I'm sorry about last night. Oh, god. I can't believe I let you carry me out of the bar like that. I thought I was dreaming, but obviously, I wasn't if I'm here with you. And I was even brazen enough to force you to spend the night with me. I'm sure the last thing you wanted was to take care of a drunk idiot. I can't—"

I covered his mouth with my hands to stop his self-deprecating ramblings. "Listen here. I'm not sorry for last night. In fact, I very much enjoyed sleeping with you in my arms. It'd be like that every night if I had any say."

Caleb couldn't look me in the eye. He hung his head and used his hand to shield himself from my view, probably covering the blush that I knew was creeping up his neck. I gave him a kiss on the top of his head and hopped off the bed.

"Why don't you wash up and I'll make breakfast? There's a spare toothbrush on the counter for you." I'd let him hide this time. I didn't want to overwhelm him all at once. But he better believe we were having a talk soon to discuss the new changes in our relationship. I wanted to ask him why he'd claimed me in front of Alfie last night. Was he jealous because he felt the same way I did?

Caleb came out of the bedroom freshly washed and, to my disappointment, with pants on. He grabbed his glasses off the kitchen counter where I'd placed them after we fell asleep on the couch the other night. I plated the eggs and bacon and placed them on the dining table. Caleb followed behind me carrying forks.

"So, what do you want for dinner tonight?" I watched Caleb dig into his food like he hadn't eaten in years. He paused when he heard my question and shrugged. I continued, "Well, I thought maybe we could talk at dinner tonight." I knew we didn't have time this morning as Caleb had to get ready to leave for his mom's place. He told me he usually picked up groceries for his family before brunch, and he still needed to shower before he left.

Caleb nodded but didn't say anything. We ate the rest of breakfast in silence, both having a lot on our minds. It wasn't an awkward silence, but more of the comforting silence of those so used to being around each other that they didn't have the constant need to fill the air with words.

Hours later, I finished making dinner and kept it warm in the oven. Caleb would be coming over any minute now, and my heart was thumping very obnoxiously in my chest. I wanted to talk with him about our relationship and where it might lead, but first, I wanted to tell him about the bakery. I spent most of the day compiling all the data I gathered and putting it in the binder for him to see. I hoped this would dispel any doubts he had about running the bakery because I knew he could do it and succeed. I just hoped he didn't get mad at me for stepping on his toes.

Caleb walked in a minute later carrying a plate of cookies. The door was now left unlocked for him since he came over every night. He set the plate down on the kitchen counter and came to sit next to me on the couch.

His soft "hi" made me break out in a wide grin. He didn't blush when he said it anymore, but it still gave me a secret thrill. He looked at the binder in my hand and gave me a curious glance. "What's that?"

I gave the binder to him and braced myself for any anger that he may have. "I, uh, did some research about what you would need to open a bakery. I found state and federal grants that you could apply for and low-interest loans. I also compiled data on local bakeries and their estimated profits so you know what you're dealing with. Actually, Osona was kind enough to help me with that."

Caleb slowly flipped through the pages in the binder and skimmed through the papers.

"Osona also said that she'd be willing to sell the bakery to you if you passed her test. She's also willing to work out a deal with you if you don't have the funds right now." His head shot up, and he gaped.

"You...you did all of this?"

I nodded. "Are you mad?" I asked hesitantly. "I'm sorry if I overstepped, but I don't want you giving up on your dream just because—"

Caleb lunged at me and stopped the rest of my sentence with his mouth. I froze for a second before pulling him tighter and returning his kiss. He wasn't the best kisser, but his clumsy enthusiasm worked me up in ways no one else ever had. I threaded my fingers through his hair as I savored his taste, forgetting about everything around us.

When the air was sucked completely out of my lungs, I nudged him off me and laid my forehead on his. We stayed like that for a couple minutes, both catching our breath like we'd just run a marathon. Caleb leaned forward again and placed a gentle peck on my lips. I could see the hunger in his eyes as we stared at each other, and I knew he wanted to take the kiss further. I put some distance between us before he lured me on that path and I lost all my senses to him.

"Wait." I sat up straight but rested my hands on his shoulders so that we were still touching. "I need to know that if we do this, it won't ruin our friendship. I want you so damn bad, but I can't imagine not having you in my life."

He raised a hand and cupped my cheek, then leaned in for another peck. "I can't imagine my life without you either. I want this. I want you. God, I've wanted you since the moment I met you, but I need you to know that I'm not good at this." He waved his hand between us and hesitated before admitting, "I've never been in a relationship before."

It was my turn to give him the deer-in-the-headlights look. I couldn't believe that such an amazing and sweet man like Caleb had never been in a relationship before, and warmth surged through my heart knowing that he was willing to give it a try with me.

"Don't get me wrong," he interjected. "I'm not a virgin or anything. I just...don't do relationships. I'm awkward at best when it comes to emotions, and I don't know how to mix my personal life and my sex life. I tend to push people away when there are hints of something *more*, but I don't want that with you. I...I want..." The rest of his words caught in his throat. He stared meaningfully at me, trying to convey something. I understood. He didn't need to say it out loud.

"Shh. It's okay." I grabbed his hands and leaned our foreheads together again. "I suck at relationships too. We can learn how to be in one together. Don't we make quite the pair?"

Caleb let out a soft chuckle, filled with a mixture of amusement and relief. He grabbed me and used his kisses to tell me just how much he wanted me, wanted *this*, whatever this was. Heck if I knew, but I was ready to explore and find out. But first...

I broke off the kiss again and pulled him to his feet. "Let's take this to the bedroom. I don't want to corrupt Lady's eyes." We glanced at the cat tree in the corner of the room where Lady sat at the top staring at us. Her crescent eyes glared at us with judgment. We burst out laughing when she turned her head in a little "humph."

"We wouldn't want that," Caleb joked. He started toward my room and pulled me along as if I wouldn't follow him to wherever the hell he wanted. He could kidnap me right now, and I would be willing to do anything to make him happy.

I closed my door and locked it for good measure since Lady recently learned how to open doors. She was smarter than some people I knew.

I dragged Caleb to the bed we'd slept in together just that morning and pushed him back onto the black sheets. We were both wearing way too many clothes. I remedied that by taking off my shirt with one swoop and stepping out of my pants. My boxers stayed on for now because I had some exploring to do first.

Caleb quickly threw off his shirt as well and shimmied out of his pants. I could only see the outline of his body in the dark room, and that wouldn't do. Not at all. I had to see his beautiful skin and the sweet blushes I was determined to elicit all over his body.

"Can I turn on the table lamp? You're so beautiful. I want to see all of you," I asked. I knew some people didn't like having sex with the lights on, and I respected that. However, I hoped to god that he said yes because I couldn't get the sight of his beautiful pale skin against my dark sheets out of my mind.

He paused for a bit, shocked still by the question, before nodding in assent. I could feel my face breaking out into a huge grin, and I might have done a little happy dance. I prayed it was too dark for Caleb to see, but the soft chuckle he let out told me my prayers had gone unanswered.

Pretending like nothing had happened, I crawled over him to turn on the lamp on the nightstand, and then I scooted back to get a good look at the feast laid out before me. It was just how I fantasized. The dim lamplight bounced off his pale skin and illuminated the blush forming on his neck. He was breathtaking. He would look even better in the natural light, but I had plenty of time for that later.

Caleb squirmed under my intense gaze, covering his red face. I wasn't going to let him hide behind his hands. I grabbed both his hands in one of mine and brought them over his head. I leaned down and devoured his mouth, making sure to suck his lips, reddening them to the color of roses.

I trailed soft kisses down his chin and neck, taking small nibbles but making sure I didn't leave a mark where others could see. I loved leaving my mark to claim what was mine, but a lot of men found it vulgar, and I didn't want to scare Caleb away on our first night. However, all bets were off on the skin that was usually hidden underneath his clothes.

"God, you're so beautiful." I sucked one of his pink nubs in my mouth, making sure to thoroughly abuse it with my tongue. Caleb's breath hitched, and he squirmed even more underneath me. "You like that, huh?" I used my hand to play with his other nipple. It perked up under my touch, and the skin around it was marred pink.

"Zack," he gasped. "I...I want..." He lifted his bottom off the bed and ground his cock against mine. There were too many layers between us, and I had to fix that.

I released his hands and attacked his mouth once more. I would give him exactly what he wanted, but I'd have my fun first.

When I pulled away from the kiss, Caleb's eyes were glazed as he lay there in nothing but his briefs and glasses. I trailed kisses down his skin again and gave a kiss over his cloth-covered dick before pulling them off. I was right. He was pink everywhere. Even his dick was a pretty pink color that matched the blush that blossomed all over his skin.

I laid kisses all over the area around his crotch, but purposefully avoided his dick. He wiggled under my kisses and his hands moved to form a tight grip on my hair. My mouth landed on his inner thigh, and I finally allowed myself to leave a single mark there. I leaned back to admire my work. His whole body was splotched with pink, and the hickey I'd left on his inner thigh was an especially stark contrast against his pale skin. His angry dick was leaking precum and demanding attention, but I didn't want him to come until I was snuggled deep within him.

I lifted his legs over my shoulders so that I was aligned to his hole and ground my boxer-covered dick against him, and he groaned. His cock twitched, and more precum drizzled down his ass. I was going to have to change my bedding after this, and it would be so worth it.

"Goddammit, Zack. Hurry the fuck up," Caleb moaned in frustration. He sat up and scrambled to get my boxers off before taking off his glasses and placing them on the nightstand. I chuckled and let him do what he wanted. Once my boxers were completely off, he paused and gaped at my cock in shock. I chuckled again, leaning in to give him a soft kiss.

"We don't have to go all the way," I muttered against his skin. I knew my size was intimidating. We didn't need penetration to have sex. I was more than willing to make him moan all night in other ways.

He shook his head and tentatively grabbed the base of my cock. "I want to." Caleb didn't hesitate when he made up his mind. He pushed me to lie on my back and engulfed my cock. A groan slipped out of me at the sensation of his warm and wet mouth. I watched as he choked down my length, his face beet-red as he worked my cock. I threaded my fingers through his soft hair and enjoyed the view. When he tried to take more of me in, he gagged, tears forming at the corner of his eyes.

I pulled him off me. "Are you okay? Don't force yourself." I wiped the saliva that slipped from his mouth. His usually pale pink lips were now a cherry red. I couldn't resist the urge to suck on them.

Pulling back, he grabbed my cock again and bit his lower lip.

"Turn around. I think it'll be easier if you're on your stomach." I grabbed a pillow to put under his hips. He lay with his back facing me and his butt pointed to my face.

My mouth felt uncomfortably dry at the sight of his plump bottom. I licked my lips to try and get some moisture flowing in my mouth again. I was undoubtedly an ass man, and Caleb's bubble butt was one I could feast on for hours. I squeezed one of the thick cheeks, and he shivered under my touch.

Caleb looked back at me shyly and said, "Sorry. I know it's kinda weird, but my butt is sensitive." A strangled growl sounded from my throat. *Oh, God.* I was going to come before we even got started.

"There's nothing weird about that." I pressed a kiss to one of his milky-white ass cheeks while maintaining eye contact with him. His eyelids shuttered at my touch, and he wiggled his butt closer to get more traction. "In fact, that's the hottest thing I've ever heard."

I knew I wasn't going to last long if this kept up. I'd wanted him since I first laid eyes on him. I'd have time to tease him later, but at this moment, I needed to be inside him. Now.

I crawled up his body and leaned over to grab the lube and condoms out of my nightstand. Lubing up my fingers, I played with his twitching hole with one hand as I massaged his butt with my other. My fingers left red marks on his delicate skin that only made me want to take a bite of his bum.

So I did.

I licked and nibbled on the soft skin as I slipped one, then two fingers inside him. Caleb's moans were getting louder the longer I played with his ass. When he was used to three fingers, he turned back to glare at me. "Are you going to torture me all night? Hurry the fuck up!"

Horny Caleb was bossy. I liked it. I shot him a cheeky smirk and gave one last kiss to the cheeks I'd worked hard on making fully pink. His eyes lingered on me as I slowly tore the condom and slid it on my rock-hard cock. His stern glare told me I would be in trouble if I didn't give him what he wanted soon, and I didn't plan to disappoint.

I grabbed his ass and lifted it so he was supported by his knees. "Are you ready?" I asked.

He bit his lower lip and nodded. "Hurry."

I took my time sliding inside him, studying his expression to make sure he was okay. I wasn't easy to take in, and I didn't want to hurt him. Another groan left my lips when I bottomed out. He was tight around my thickness, and it was almost enough to do me in.

Afraid of hurting him, I gritted my teeth and waited for him to adjust. Caleb made tiny whimpers underneath me. Thinking he was in pain, I wanted to pull out, but he ground his ass closer to me before I could.

"More," he groaned.

All thoughts left my brain, and the only thing I remem-bered to do was thrust hard. I grabbed his ass and lifted it closer to make it easier to pound into him. I was so close and sure to make a fool of myself by coming first. I would make it up to him because there was no way I was going to last.

With my orgasm within reach, I kneaded both his ass cheeks hard, leaving more red marks on the pale skin. The sight of his flushed skin snapped the last of my control. Caleb's moan of pleasure filled my ears, and his channel spasmed around me in a tight grip. I groaned out my own intense pleasure as I shot inside the condom, falling on top of him as I tried to catch my breath.

"Did you just..." I already knew the answer. He'd come with his dick untouched. The thought of it made me so hot that my cock twitched again, demanding more, but I knew we didn't have the energy for another round.

"I told you my butt was sensitive," he grumbled against the mattress. I let out a soft chuckle and kissed his shoulder blade.

"You're perfect," I whispered against his ear. He shivered, and I made a mental note to find out how sensitive his ears actually were on another day. As for today, we were both thor-oughly worn out.

I held the base of the condom and slowly pulled out of him. Caleb winced and breathed a sigh of relief when I was fully out. He flipped around and sank into the mattress, his eyes already half closed.

"I'll be right back. Wait here." I gave him a quick peck on the lips before climbing off the bed.

"Oh, trust me. You couldn't pay me to move." He sunk deeper into the mattress and fully closed his eyes.

Pulling off the condom, I tied the end and threw it in the bathroom trash can. I wet a rag and quickly cleaned myself off before wetting a new rag with warm water for Caleb. Heading back to the room, I found Caleb softly snoring where I'd left him. Careful not to wake him, I cleaned him up and threw the rag in the laundry basket.

I put away our uneaten dinner and turned off the lights as I made my way back to the bedroom.

Caleb was still snoring when I rolled him under the sheet and pulled him into my arms. I pressed a kiss on his forehead and closed my eyes, feeling happier than I'd felt in years.

SEVENTEEN

CALEB

The rays of morning sun woke me. I must've forgotten to close my blinds last night. There was a warm body next to me, and I snuggled closer to hide my face from the early morning light. *Hold on...*

I blinked awake to find hard muscles laid out before my eyes. Memories of the night before rushed forward, and my mind went on red alert, telling me to flee. I tried to get up, but Zack mumbled something and tightened his hold around me. Since my escape attempt had failed, I obediently lay back down and breathed in his scent. He smelled like musk and spice that reminded me of Christmas desserts. His scent calmed me, and I discovered my desire to flee was slowly dissipating.

Zack made me feel protected, but not suffocated. He was the air that I was slowly starting to realize that I couldn't live without. I was usually too wound up after sex to fall asleep with my partner, the hamster wheel in my brain spinning until I made whatever excuse I needed to get out of there and return to the comfort of my own home.

Last night had been different. After the amazing dicking I'd received and probably the most intense orgasm ever to exist on planet Earth, I'd fallen asleep not even caring that I was covered in what was probably a pound of jizz. Zack must have cleaned me up since I didn't feel crusty.

My heart warmed at that thought. He always made sure to take care of me. He gave me comfort without making me feel like I had to explain myself. He was just there. A silent but much-needed support.

I looked up at his sleeping face. He was so beautiful. Long, black eyelashes framed his eyelids and hid what I knew to be the greenest eyes I'd ever seen. Yes, those eyes. Wait...

"Morning," Zack rasped, his voice laden with sleep.

"Morning," I peeped. I hid my face in his chest, embarrassed at being caught staring at him. His chest rumbled with a deep chuckle, and he pulled me tighter against his body.

"You smell delicious." Zack buried his face in my hair. He must have been delusional because I was sure I currently smelled of sweat and cum.

"I'm glad you didn't run away," he muttered.

"You didn't give me much of a choice. You had an octopus hold on me." Another deep chuckle rumbled through his chest.

He released his hold on me and shrugged. "Sorry, my body knows what it wants." He didn't look the least bit sorry.

Zack got off the bed and walked to his dresser. His golden skin glowed in the morning sun. Thankfully, his back was to me, or else he would have caught me staring at his ass the whole time. Even though I preferred to bottom, I wouldn't say no to an ass that fuckable. Images of me pounding into Zack floated into my head. I'd make him moan so hard and get payback for him being such a tease last night. My face heated at the memories of the previous night.

Zack put on a fresh pair of boxers and turned around at that moment. Seeing my blush, a huge smirk bloomed across his face.

"God, sweets. You're killing me. If only we didn't have work today, I'd make you scream all over again."

I groaned and covered my face with my hands. Zack walked to my side and threaded his fingers through my hair and placed a soft kiss on my head. "Go wash up. I'll make breakfast."

I lay in bed until I couldn't hear his footsteps. Afterwards, I got dressed in last night's clothes, sans underwear since they were covered in dried precum. Since Zack had dark sheets, the dried cum was clearly visible. It was a shining reminder of our activities from last night. Another blush cursed my pale skin, but this time, there was thankfully no one there to witness it.

I quickly stripped the bed and threw the dirty sheets into the laundry basket he kept in his bathroom. I didn't know where he kept his clean sheets, so I left it bare and closed the door to make sure Lady didn't roll all over his bare mattress.

"I stripped your sheets, but I don't know where you keep the clean ones," I said when I walked into the kitchen. My stomach grumbled from the scent of bacon frying on the pan. Two plates sat on the kitchen counter with a good portion of scrambled eggs on them. The toaster dinged its completion, and I grabbed the finished toast and placed two slices on each plate.

"Thanks. I'll do it later." Zack turned off the burner and divided the bacon between the two plates. We fell into our normal routine—Zack carrying the plates to the table and me following behind with the forks and drinks. It was weird to know that we'd spent so much time together that we had a routine. Weird, but nice.

We didn't say anything at first, both of us hungrily digging into our breakfast. When half our plates were eaten clean, Zack put down his fork.

He grabbed my hand and rubbed his thumb back and forth against my skin. "Do you regret last night?" he asked in a whisper, concern etched on his face.

I shook my head. "Never."

"I want you to know that this is all very new to me. I don't know what I'm doing, and I'll mess up, but what I do know is that I want to be with you."

My heart softened at his words. I couldn't imagine him lacking in confidence in anything he did, but I liked that he was in the same boat as me. "I have no idea what I'm doing either. With relationships, I mean. But we'll learn together."

He released my hand and got up from his chair. Seconds later, he was kneeling beside me and looking up at my lowered head. He cupped my face with his hands. "Does that mean you're officially my schnookums now?" He gave my face a little squeeze and rewarded me with one of his smirks.

I rolled my eyes. "You're never gonna let that go, are you?"

"Of course not. As your boyfriend, it's my right to call you whatever mushy endearments I desire." Amusement danced in his eyes, and I knew he would make it his mission to tease me endlessly with those stupid nicknames. And I wouldn't have it any other way.

We talked about the bakery for the rest of the morning. Zack patiently went over the binder with me and answered all the questions I had—there were many—without any complaint and dispelled all my concerns. He'd also found me private lenders that offered decent interest rates for startup companies.

As someone who was almost anal about organization, I was amazed by just how much work Zack had put into this binder to make the whole presentation systematic. That weird tingly feeling spread through my stomach again, and I rubbed my belly to soothe it.

Zack encouraged me to set a day to do the test with Osona. Even if I decided not to open a bakery, it was still beneficial to have someone as talented as her giving me feedback. He said he would set up a date two weeks from now so that I had time to prepare what I wanted to make.

There was still a bit of time before we had to leave for work after everything had been discussed, so we held hands and continued talking about the future. We were both hyped at what the future could bring. I loved that Zack was just as excited as I was about this venture.

He mentioned maybe leaving his job and starting off on his own as well. He looked straight at me as he talked of working side by side to achieve our dreams. His eyes had a faraway look in them, and a goofy smile appeared on his face. I squeezed his hand and imagined the future he described. I couldn't think of anything more perfect.

We said our goodbyes soon after that. Work would start soon, and we both desperately needed a shower if we didn't want to head into the office smelling like spunk. Zack held my hand at the door like he was reluctant to let me go.

"I'll see you at dinner," he said more than asked.

"Dinner," I confirmed, leaning in to give him a peck, as I was just as reluctant to go, but appeased to know we'd see each other again soon enough.

A week later, I discovered that entering this whole new relationship box with Zack wasn't much different than before. We still spent practically all our free time together and had dinner together every night. The only thing different now was that we'd added kissing into the equation, and a lot of it.

It wasn't abnormal for him to attack my mouth as soon as I walked into his apartment. That would lead to us making out on the couch until our stomachs demanded to be fed. Which led to an excruciating dinner where he teased me with his words and sometimes his foot. Which led to me dragging him to bed where he tortured me with his touches and kisses until I begged him to fuck me.

Needless to say, I'd never been more well-fucked than I had been in the last week. Mom mentioned how I looked different this morning at brunch. I didn't feel any different, but that might have been because I was being fucked out of my mind that I didn't have time to worry about the stress of work.

At brunch, I told Conner and my mom about the test Zack had set up for me. They were both supportive of my decision and asked numerous questions in their excitement for me. I made vegan lemon bars for them to try and packed extra in a bag for Conner to take on his trip tomorrow. I'd been testing out new recipes and experimenting with my own all week. Zack had been my guinea pig, but he was a horrible critic. He would just keep singing praises of everything I made and found no fault in them.

I smiled at the thought of how he'd almost made himself sick eating a whole pan of Malva pudding. There was a tingling in the back of my head like someone was staring at me, and I turned around to see my mom giving me a knowing smile.

"Did you get chewed on by a bug?" Conner asked from the other side of me, pointing at the exposed skin by the base of my shoulder.

I quickly brought a hand up to cover the mark. "Uh, yep. Dang mosquito season. They're all coming out now. I, uh, should go put on some ointment and a band-aid." I shot out of my seat and ran to the bathroom. I pulled my collar away from my shoulder to reveal a tiny bruise Zack had left on me last night.

Another thing I'd learned about him was that he loved leaving marks on me with his mouth, and I secretly loved it as well. It was a mark of ownership that made me feel claimed and like he was always with me. He didn't usually leave the hickeys in places that could be seen, but last night had been intense.

My face heated as I remembered how Zack had teased my butt last night until it was tender and red. My angry cock leaked enough precum to soak the sheets before Zack finally took me. I was coming before the second thrust, and he stayed still inside me, nibbling on my shoulders until I was ready for round two.

"Caleb, you done in there?" I jumped at the sound of my mom's voice and scrambled to cover the hickey on my shoulder with a band-aid.

"Yeah, coming." I straightened my collar to make sure nothing was out of place before opening the door. My mom stood outside the door with her arms crossed.

"I want to meet him."

"W-Wha...Who are you..."

"Don't give me that, Caleb William Turner. I've never seen you as happy as you've been these past couple of weeks. You're bringing him to our brunch date next week. I need to make sure that he's treating my boy right."

"Mom," I groaned as I ran my hand through my hair. "Please no. It's super new, and you'll scare him away."

"What's there to be scared of? It's just three grown adults getting brunch and mimosas together. It'll be a blast. Now, come on. Conner made a list of what he liked and didn't like about the lemon bars."

That was how I knew Conner was my little brother. He loved lists almost as much as I did.

Hours later as I snuggled with Zack in his bed—I hadn't spent a night in my own apartment since we'd gotten together—I told him about my mom wanting to have brunch together.

"Do you think she'll like me?" he whispered in my hair. He loved holding me in his arms.

"She'll adore you," I replied, meaning every word of it. In the time that I had known Zack, he'd shown what an amazing human being he was. He was kind and patient and funny and sweet. He'd become essential to me like baking was. The voices in my head telling me all the horrible things that could go wrong every second of the day quieted in his presence. He literally chased them away. "Just like I do," I whispered the last part into his hard chest.

His arms tightened around me, and I rested my forehead on his chest to feel the thumping of his heartbeat.

"I adore you too." His deep voice reverberated through my body as he continued whispering sweet nothings into my hair, and I was eventually lulled into a deep sleep, safe in his arms.

"Caleb, over here." Mom waved at us from her table, three mimosas already waiting for us. Zack's grip on my hand tightened. His hands were sweatier than normal.

"She'll love you," I assured him as we walked to her table. Mom got up from her seat to give me a hug before turning to Zack.

"It's nice to meet you, Mrs. Turner. My name's Zack." He reached his hand out for a handshake. Mom ignored the hand and leaned to give him a hug instead.

"Please call me Maryann. It's so good to meet the man who's turned my boy into such a sap."

"Mom! I thought we said we weren't going to embarrass me today," I said through gritted teeth. This was exactly why I didn't want them to meet yet. Mom had too much ammunition against me, and she wasn't afraid to use it, and I knew she'd say something that would have Zack running from me like I was an alien with six eyes.

"Oh, honey. You're being overdramatic again." She led Zack to the seat beside her and handed him one of the mimosas. "So, are you a native of Corio City? Caleb mentioned you moved to his apartment building last month."

I sat down across from her and signaled her with my eyes, begging her not to say anything more to embarrass me. She ignored me, of course.

"Caleb said you were handsome, but now I can see why he was absolutely smitten when you moved in next door." I groaned and slammed my head on the table. Kill me now.

Zack looked at me with an eyebrow raised and chuckled. "Did he now? Well, I'm absolutely smitten with him as well." He grabbed my hand and gave it a squeeze.

Maybe bringing him to brunch hadn't been such a bad idea.

"And to answer your previous question, Mrs. Turner—"

"Maryann," Mom insisted.

"Maryann. I came to Corio City for college and never left." The waitress came to drop off the menus, and Zack passed them to us. We were silent while we decided our food choice.

"What are you getting, sweets?" Zack asked over his menu.

"The Eggs Benedict sound good, but so does the salmon toast." I was terrible at making decisions, especially when it came to food. It was hard to choose when you wanted to eat everything.

"How about you get the Benedict, and I'll get the toast?

Then we can share." My heart lay on the ground in a pile of goo. This man couldn't get any more perfect. I could tell Mom agreed with my inner thoughts from the wide grin she tried to hide behind her glass.

The waitress came back to bring a round of ice waters and took our orders. Mom leaned on the table with her head resting on her hands and turned to Zack again. "Do you have any siblings?"

"Nope, it's just me. The world wouldn't be able to handle two Miller siblings." Zack tried to pass it off as a joke, but I could tell by the strain in his voice that he was uncomfortable. I tried to signal to my mom to change the conversation, but she ignored me once again.

"What about your parents? Are you close?"

A vein throbbed on his right temple. I usually loved seeing that vein because it meant he was so turned on that he'd lost control of his sexual desire. But not today. I didn't want to see it if it meant he was tormented by a past that obviously lived rent-free in his mind.

"No, uh, we're not close." I squeezed his hand in silent support. He'd told me before that he wasn't close with his parents, and I had asked him why one night while we were in bed. He simply told me they never wanted him. It was one of the only nights he'd allowed me to cuddle him to sleep instead of the other way around.

"Oh, I'm sorry for bringing it up." Concern etched Mom's face, and she laid a comforting hand on his shoulder.

"It's fine. It's not a sob story or anything. I was the unex-pected child they never wanted. They didn't have room for me in their lives. They were too absorbed with each other." Zack laid his other hand on top of mine and rubbed his thumb against the back of my hand. I knew it was his way of comforting himself. "They never mistreated me," he quickly added. "They provided everything to make sure I was comfortable. They were just...absent in my life, and when I came out to them in college, my conservative parents made it clear it would be better if we cut each other out of our lives."

My heart broke hearing what his parents had said to him. The desire to hold him and shield him from the evils of the worlds welled up inside me.

How could anyone not want Zack? The kind man who cooked dinner for me every night because he knew I hated cooking. The man who ordered salmon, even though he preferred bacon, just because I wanted to eat it. His parents were idiots. They'd done a good job providing for him so that he could become the man he was today, but they were idiots for not wanting this amazing man in their lives.

Mom wiped away the tears lingering on the corner of her eyes. "Well, you have us now, and I insist you come to Sunday Brunch from now on. You'll be able to meet Conner next weekend since he'll be back from his trip Saturday night." She glanced at me, and I knew I wasn't going to like what she was about to say. "It'll probably be for the best since Caleb's mind is always wandering these days during brunch like he's missing a certain someone. Perhaps with you there, he'll finally leave his head and stay present in the real world."

I groaned again. Brunch was a bad idea. Terrible idea. And I was reminded just how bad an idea this was when they began trading stories. Mom told Zack of the time I followed a random woman a couple years ago, thinking it was her. I was lost in thought and trailed after her to the car. I probably would have gotten in the car too, even though it was a different color and make than the one Mom drove, if not for the woman screaming bloody Mary, thinking I was stalking her.

Zack in turn regaled her with the tale from the other night when we'd been cuddling on the couch watching TV. Well, he was watching TV, and I was imagining recipes that I could try in order to find the perfect dessert to give Osona.

"He kept nodding and agreeing to all the ridiculous things I said. And when I told him I was an alien from Mars, he said no wonder I was so hot." My face burned at the thought of my mom finding out I thought aliens were hot. Their laughter filled the table, and I was happy they got along like old friends, even if it was at my expense.

EIGHTEEN
ZACK

Osona agreed to meet us Wednesday evening since that was their slow day. Caleb had been baking nonstop almost every night this past week, and I was all for it, made evident by the small paunch that now covered my abs. He'd been so worried about the test that he'd made enough sweets to feed the whole building. The two older ladies who lived together on the first floor came by more than once to drop off empty plates from the desserts Caleb had given them. Heck, even Noah, the recluse from the unit across from mine, dropped by multiple times for a sugar hit. One thing they all had in common was that they left happy.

I knew Caleb would kill the test, but he was a nervous wreck as we walked into the bakery. He was carrying a tray of the desserts he'd prepared, so I put my arm around his waist to comfort him.

"Hey. You're gonna do great." He didn't look convinced but nodded anyway.

Osona was waiting for us at the counter when we walked in. "Zack, so good to see you." She got off the stool by the register and came around the counter to give me a hug. "And this must be Caleb," she said, turning to Caleb. She took the container from his hand and placed it on the counter behind her before turning back to wrap her arms around him.

"H-hi," he squeaked out. He looked comically squished by the woman half his size. When Osona finally released him, he seemed a bit off-kilter, but didn't say anything.

"Let's head to the back." She picked up the container and led us to the little employee break room and pointed to the couch. "Sit down. I'll make some tea. It'll help calm your nerves."

Caleb shot her a grateful smile. When she left the tiny room, he leaned his head on the back of the couch and let out a sigh. I sat next to him and wrapped him in my arms. "You're gonna do great."

He leaned his head in the nook of my shoulder and took a deep breath. He'd told me before that my scent calmed him down.

"I like her. She seems nice and like a no-nonsense kind of woman." I smiled at his assessment. In the years I'd known Osona, I never knew her to take the easy way out. When she set her mind on something, she did it. The woman had built a successful business and had kept it running through the change of time. And most importantly, she knew when to ask for help if she needed it.

Osona came back with a tray of tea and sat on the chair on the other side of the wall. She asked Caleb about his baking and how he'd gotten into it. Caleb answered her questions and told her how ingenious the creations she'd made were, which led to a lengthy discussion on different recipes they'd tried and changes they'd made to improve them.

I watched Caleb come to life during the discussion. He animatedly waved his hands around as he talked. He could barely sit still. My smile was probably as deep as his as I watched him. I loved seeing him in his element. Baking was what he was meant to do.

"We should try your dessert," Osona said half an hour later. "I'll get it from the fridge."

"I'll help you," Caleb offered, getting up to follow her.

I checked my phone while they were gone. Eric had sent me a text about the hookup he'd had last night. He was almost certain that they were certifiably crazy. I didn't miss those days. Some people weren't satisfied unless they had a different person in bed every night, but that wasn't me. At least not anymore. I loved knowing that I had a special someone to take care of and who in turn was there for me when I needed him.

They came back a couple minutes later with a tray of plated desserts. Caleb had made some sort of fruit tart with a pale green-colored filling. I didn't even ask him what it was before taking a bite of the treat, knowing that everything he made was delicious.

My eyes flitted closed with pleasure as the flavor exploded in my mouth. Osona also made a noise of delight next to me.

"This must be matcha!" she exclaimed. She brought a hand to cover her mouth, her eyes widening. "I've never thought to make a fruit tart with a matcha base, but you clearly know what you're doing."

Caleb nodded, a flush forming on his face from her compliment. "Some fruit tarts can be overly sweet. I thought the matcha would balance it out and enhance the flavor of the fruits."

Osona nodded in agreement. She took another bite and closed her eyes to enjoy it. "Yes, the slightly bitter taste of the matcha perfectly complements the filling and fruits. It's the perfect treat for older people like me who don't enjoy too much sweetness." She gave Caleb a wink, making him blush some more.

"Well, I know I've made my decision. You've passed the test with flying colors. You're very skilled at your craft, my dear." She put her finished plate on the table and used a napkin to wipe the crumbs off her mouth.

"Really?" Caleb's eyes widened. He stared in a daze for a second before shaking himself out of it. "I...Thank you. You don't know what this means to me."

A glint of understanding flickered in her eyes. "I'll be relieved to know that the bakery will be left to someone capable. It's done a lot for us, and it breaks my heart to think the shop could fall into ruin one day." She looked around the tiny room, looking at spots that held nothing but memories of her past.

"I...I don't have the funds to buy the business outright from you," Caleb lowered his head and fiddled with his fingers.

Osona laid a hand on his again. "Some things are more important than money. My family isn't lacking financially. What we care about more is knowing that this place will be in good hands. The rest we can work out."

We spent another hour discussing the transfer process, and Osona went over what needed to be repaired in the bakery. Caleb wanted to renovate the place before holding a grand reopening. Osona graciously allowed Caleb to do a payment plan to slowly purchase the business. He would rent the space at the low price they offered until he was ready to buy the building from them. He would still have to get a loan to afford the renovations and daily expenditures of the business, but he was so close to finally making his dream come true.

We left the place with hugs and a container full of sweets Osona had given us. Caleb had a huge smile pasted on his face as he gushed about how kind Osona was and the big plans he had for the place. I took one of his hands while holding the container with the other. An equally large grin spread across my face.

"Lady, come eat." I poked her as she lay on the cat tree with her eyes closed. Her ears flickered when she heard my voice, but she didn't open her eyes at my touch.

Caleb walked up behind me. The sweets he made for game night were waiting on a plate on the counter.

"Is she okay? It's not like her to not finish breakfast either." Lady let out a weak meow when he stroked her body, but her eyes remained closed.

"Should we take her to the vet?" he asked, his brows furrowed in worry.

I shook my head. I didn't want to believe Lady was sick, and if we took her to the vet, it would be too real. "I'll stay home and watch her. You go to game night."

"I'll stay home with you. Just let me drop off the desserts first." My heart warmed at him calling this place his home. Little traces of him had slowly popped up around the apartment. Heck, most of his baking supplies had already migrated to the kitchen here.

"No, you go have fun. Tell the boys I'm sorry I can't make it this week." Both of us didn't need to be here. He spent most of his time with me, so he should go enjoy game night with his friends.

The frown on his face deepened. "Are you sure? They'll be fine with me missing one week."

I hooked my arms around his neck and pulled him in for a deep kiss. "I love that you care so much, Caleb. You have so much kindness in you." I sprinkled small pecks all over his face before landing one more on his lips. "Don't worry. I'll come get you if anything happens. Go have fun."

Caleb was reluctant to leave, but I grabbed the dessert plate and shoved him out of the apartment with it.

"Fine, but you have to get me if you need me. For *anything*." He leaned in for one more kiss before turning to Will and Jason's unit.

"Beat their asses for me." He gave me a thumbs up as he walked into their apartment. I closed the door once he was gone and turned back to Lady.

"It's just you and me, old girl." I grabbed her off the cat tree and placed her by her food bowl. She finally took a couple bites after a bit of coaxing but went back to lying with her eyes closed after.

"All right, we can cuddle on the couch and watch TV for a bit, but you have to eat more after that, okay?" I picked her up again and carried her to the couch. She felt a bit warm, but she was also covered with what seemed like ten pounds of fur, so I didn't think anything of it.

I put something on in the background as I continued to stroke Lady. Thirty minutes later, I noticed that her breathing sped up, and she was shivering.

"Lady?" I shook her a bit, but she didn't respond. Her body felt a lot hotter than before. "Lady!" I tried again. My voice hitched to the pitch of adolescent teen girls. Panic seized through me at the thought of something terrible happening to her. I shot up and ran out of my apartment to get Caleb. I slammed the door open and ran into the room. Four pairs of eyes stared at me in my panicked state.

"Caleb, Lady...she..." I couldn't get the words out. If anything happened to Lady, it would be all my fault. I should have known she was sick and taken her to the vet earlier.

Caleb turned to his friends and apologized for having to

leave in the middle of the game. They told him to go and looked at me with concern.

"Hey, look at me." Caleb's soft voice was a beacon that tethered me to the present. "It's going to be okay." He held me tight, letting me go only after I stopped shivering. He grabbed my hand and led me back to my apartment. "Why don't you put on some shoes, and I'll put Lady in her carrier?"

I looked down at my feet and realized I was only in my socks. I had run out of my apartment without putting any shoes on. I must've looked like a madman in front of our friends. I quickly chucked on a random pair of sneakers and waited in the hall. Caleb came out soon after with the carrier in his hands.

"You're in no state to drive," he said when we reached the parking lot. I followed him to his car and sat in the passenger seat. Caleb handed me Lady's carrier before walking around to the driver's seat. He did a quick search on his phone and called the closest twenty-four-hour emergency vet clinic and quickly explained the situation. When he got confirmation to bring her in, Caleb pulled up the GPS and drove according to the directions of the robotic voice. The fifteen-minute drive felt like hours. I kept stroking Lady to assure her that I was there with her. She kept shivering under my touch like she couldn't chase the cold away.

Caleb dropped me off at the entrance, and I ran inside the small building. The receptionist looked up from her computer and gave me a gentle smile.

"We called just now about my cat. Please help her." The woman got out of her seat and led me to a small exam room.

"The vet will be in shortly," she said, gesturing for me to sit.

"My boyfriend is parking the car. Can you please lead him here when he comes in?"

"Of course." She gave me another smile as she shut the

door. I sat there with Lady's carrier on my lap, afraid that if I wasn't touching her, something terrible would happen to her. Her breathing was shallow now, and the heat radiating off her tiny body felt hotter than it had before.

Caleb walked into the room a couple minutes later. "Did the doctor check her yet?"

I shook my head. He came to sit next to me and put an arm around me. "It'll be okay," He whispered comforting words into my ear.

The doctor came in moments later. "Hello. My name is Wyatt Clark. I heard Lady here isn't feeling well?" He grabbed the carrier and set it on the exam table in the middle of the room.

"Let's see what's happening with her. I was told she's barely eaten all day?" He put on a pair of gloves and let Lady out of the carrier. She barely even blinked when he picked her up, even though she didn't like strangers.

"Yes, Dr. Clark. She usually begs for more food, but she barely ate half her bowl this morning." Caleb squeezed my hand for support. I glanced down at my poor baby girl lying on the cold metal table. I'd never seen her this vulnerable before. Not even when she was a stray kitten who probably hadn't had food in days. Even then, she had determination in her eyes. Not now, though.

"I'd like to do more tests with her in the back. Is that okay?" Dr. Clark asked after a few minutes of examining Lady.

"Yes, of course. I don't care how much it costs. Please do whatever you can to help her." He smiled at my words, then left to do the tests on Lady.

I collapsed back into the chair, my head hanging down between my arms. "What if she's sick and doesn't recover? If... If anything happens to her, it'll be all my fault. I should've listened when you said to take her to the vet earlier."

Caleb wrapped me into a bear hug, gently patting on my back. "Shh, it'll be okay. Lady is in good hands with Dr. Clark." "She picked me. She chose me to be her human, and now I've let her down. How could I do that to her after everything she's done for me?" My voice choked at the end, tiny sobs spilling from my lips. Caleb held me tight and whispered assurances in my ear. "She saved me, you know? The day she found me, I mean."

"Tell me about it." His voice was soft and comforting, soothing the memories of my struggles during my first year of college. Coming from a small, conservative town, sexuality was black-and-white. You were either normal or an outcast. And no one ever chose to be an outcast.

"I was in college. I hadn't talked to my parents in months, so I called my mom. I tried to tell her how college was going, but she kept leading the conversation back to her and the recent trip she'd gone on with my dad. I just...I don't know...I wanted her to take an interest in me, to give a shit about me for once in her life. So, I told her I was gay." I'd been sitting on a bench in the park during the call. Gloomy clouds had loomed above me, threatening to release their fury onto the world. I already knew what her reaction would be, but I still had a glimmer of hope in my heart. I had been so foolish.

Caleb's arms tightened around me. The comfort of them gave me the courage to continue the story.

"She told me it would be best if we went our separate ways and hung up on me. I just sat on that bench and stared into space even after it started pouring. I knew my parents had never cared about me, but I thought they cared enough to feel some sort of emotion about my coming out, even if it was anger. I was wrong. They were indifferent to my existence like I was a stranger they once crossed paths with. I could pretend it wasn't true when it wasn't said out loud, but she broke any illusions I had that day. It was confirmed—no one wanted me. I was a waste in the world. No one needed me. Then Lady came up to me and demanded I take care of her. Right then, while I sat on a bench in the pouring rain, she came up to me. She was such a tiny thing, covered in mud and filth. She was so skinny I could see her ribs. At that moment, she picked me. She needed me, and that's what kept me going. What am I going to do if something happens to her? What will I do without her?" I was hysterical now. My vision blurred with tears.

Caleb gently peeled me off his shoulder. Tears also streamed down his face, but he ignored them and stared straight in my eyes. "She's not the only one. I need you as well."

We'd never said those three little words out loud, but I could see them in his eyes. His gaze spoke of love and promises that I never dared to hope for. A future shone in his eyes, one full of comfort and family. Of being needed, but also cared for. Of having a place to finally belong.

"Lady will be okay," he said in a firm voice that left no room for questioning. "She's a fighter. She'll get better, and then we'll take her back home with us."

I kept silent and nodded because there was nothing else to say. Lady would be all right. She'd get better, and we'd be able to go back. To our home.

Dr. Clark returned to the room an hour later with a smile on his face. "Lady is doing well. She has a slight fever and is a bit dehydrated, but we fed her some antibiotics and put her on an IV. We'd like to keep her overnight to monitor her, but she should be ready to go home tomorrow morning."

Guilt rushed through me. I never should have let her interact with the unknown cat when we took our walk. This was all my fault.

"These things happen. Don't beat yourself up over it. The important thing is you brought her here in time." Dr. Clark must've seen something on my face since he tried to comfort me. "If you follow me, you can say goodnight to her before you leave."

We followed Dr. Clark to the back room where they had large cages lined up on the back wall. He opened a cage to the left and stepped aside to let us see her. Lady was sleeping soundly inside. She wasn't shivering anymore, and her breathing had returned to normal. I gave her a light pat on her back, glad to feel that she wasn't burning up like she had been earlier.

"Lady, rest well. We'll be back tomorrow morning bright and early to take you home, okay?" Her ear twitched in her sleep at the sound of my voice. Caleb said his goodnights as well. We went back to the front where we paid the bill, and the woman from earlier made an appointment for us to pick Lady up tomorrow.

We were silent on the drive home, and I might have broken down again if not for Caleb's warm hand holding mine. I was still in a daze of worry and guilt that something might have happened to Lady because of me. Caleb dragged me to our apartment and into the bathroom. He turned on the shower and stripped off my clothes.

"I...I don't think I can tonight." My voice cracked. More guilt ate at me at the thought of disappointing Caleb as well tonight.

"Shh, I know. It's okay." His soft voice echoed in the bathroom. "Let me take care of you." And he did. He led me under the warm spray and massaged my hair with shampoo. I closed my eyes and enjoyed the feeling of his hands as he washed my body until I was almost limp under his touch. When he finished rinsing me off, he wrapped me in a fluffy towel and led me to the sink.

"Brush your teeth. I'm gonna wash really quick." And so I

did. My brain wasn't functioning enough to make decisions right now, so I was more than happy to follow his directions. Caleb came up behind me with a towel wrapped around his waist. He grabbed the hair dryer and ran his fingers through my hair as he slowly dried it. My eyes closed of their own accord, knowing that I was warm and safe.

Caleb's chuckle had me blinking my eyes open again. "Don't fall asleep here. Look, the toothpaste is dripping." I looked in the mirror, and sure enough, a trail of white foam was dripping down my chin. I quickly rinsed my mouth and cleaned up the mess I'd made.

"Go to bed. I'll be right there." The hair dryer turned on again as I walked back to our bedroom. I lay on my side, eyes looking past the bathroom doorframe, where I could see Caleb's profile. I couldn't believe how lucky I was to have found a caring man as sweet as he was. And boy, was he sweet.

He finished drying his hair and proceeded to brush his teeth. He gave me a huge grin when he caught me staring, and I probably had a goofy smile on my face in return. Once he finished his nighttime routine, he walked around to his side of the bed and hugged me. I usually preferred holding him in my arms, but tonight, this was exactly what I needed. I placed a hand over his and snuggled closer to his body. He gave me a soft kiss on the back of my neck. "Goodnight. Sweet dreams, Zack," he whispered.

"Goodnight," I sleepily mumbled as I drifted off to sleep, knowing that I'd have the best dreams with him by my side.

NINETEEN

CALEB

We were at the emergency veterinary clinic early the next morning. A different woman than the one from the night before helped process Lady's discharge papers. Lady was back to her energetic self and meowed nonstop at us. The woman said they'd fed her that morning, so she wasn't crying for food. A giddy feeling grew in my heart imagining that she'd just missed us and that was the reason for the chatter this morning.

When we got home, Lady sprinted out of her carrier and zoomed around the apartment like she'd been gone for years instead of a single night. When she was satisfied to find that nothing had changed in her absence, she came back to rub herself all over Zack and me.

Zack headed to the kitchen to start breakfast while I took my laptop to the couch. Lady curled up next to me, purring her pleasure at returning to her spot. I opened up a new document on my laptop and typed out a draft resignation letter. I was going to put in my two weeks today.

Osona had kept in touch with me after the test, and we'd worked out the finer details of the business transfer. She and her husband wanted to retire ages ago but were reluctant to close the bakery permanently. That was why they were eager to do the transfer as soon as possible.

Over the past week, I'd made a checklist of everything I needed to do for the business and slowly worked on it. I looked into small business loan programs and applied to a couple with Zack's help. They were still in the process of being reviewed, but Zack was confident that I had a high probability of being approved. Osona agreed to start the transfer once I got approved for the loans. Then we'd close the bakery for the renovations and hopefully have the grand reopening before fall. Zack was also helping me with all the permits I would need to operate the bakery and the ones I'd need for the renovation.

I turned my head to the man who'd made all this possible. He was the one who'd introduced me to Osona and persuaded me to let go of my fears to pursue my dream. I saved my finished resignation letter and sent it to my email to print at work. Zack was making pancakes at the stove. I crept up behind him, wrapped my arms around his stomach, and leaned my head on his shoulder.

"What's wrong?" He turned his head slightly to look at me, his face clear of worry lines now that Lady was back home and recovered.

"Nothing." I turned my head and gave his neck a kiss. "Everything is perfect. You're perfect."

He rubbed his head against mine and resumed cooking while I stayed glued to his back. After breakfast, I gave Zack a kiss goodbye and headed to work while he took a personal day since he was worried about leaving Lady home alone.

I drove to work singing the lyrics of being Unwritten, hopeful and ready to leave the job that ate away at my soul and start living my dream. Once I turned in my resignation and finished my last two weeks, I would start my career as a professional baker. I sang louder as the reality of it hit me, and a huge grin formed on my face. It was real.

On Sunday morning, Zack and I had our morning run to the lighthouse. We sat on our usual bench and let the sea breeze cool us before heading back. I couldn't believe how far we'd come since our first jog together. I should have known Zack would mean something different to me when I felt comfortable enough to leave a trail of mucus on his shirt as I sobbed that day.

The morning sun made Zack's slick skin glisten. If I were a sculptor, he would be my muse.

"God, don't look at me like that." He playfully turned my head so I wasn't looking at him. "We don't have time for that. We gotta get groceries and head to your mom's."

He was right, of course. Even if I wanted to strip him here and claim him in the most intimate way for the world to see, we didn't have time, and I was sure Zack didn't want to stink of cum at his first official Sunday brunch with us.

I turned my head and kissed the hand that still caressed my face. A devious smirk formed on his lips, and his eyes glinted with promises of torture in the most amazing way later tonight. After brunch, of course.

The jog back home helped to relieve some of the sexual tension. I decided to shower in my own apartment because I knew that if we got naked together, being late to brunch would be more of a question of *how late* rather than the mere possibility of it.

I noticed that my shower lacked most of my bathing items, as they had been moved to Zack's place. Since my favorite bar of lavender soap wasn't here, I did a quick wash with the random bottle of body wash that was left here.

Ten minutes later, we arrived at the grocery store I usually went to before heading to Mom's. Zack pushed the cart while I threw in weekly items they used as well as the things Conner asked me for. Zack studied the two different fruit platters the grocery store had available, eventually picking the one he liked best, and placed it in the cart. I told him he didn't have to bring anything to Sunday brunch, but he insisted.

After checking out and packing the groceries in the car, we drove the rest of the way to my mom's house. Conner sat on the front stoop, playing on his phone. He lifted his head when our car pulled into the driveway. When I opened the car door, he crashed into me in a huge hug. "Hey, kid. How did the competition go? And why are you waiting outside?"

He shrugged. "It went well. Mom said you were bringing your boyfriend today."

Zack came around the car to meet us, unfazed by the daggers Conner glared his way. "Nice to meet you. I'm Zack." He reached out for a handshake.

Conner ignored it and instead said, "I know how to make killer robots."

"Conner!" I reprimanded. I made a mental note to check his robot stash and make sure none of them were of the stabby or homicidal variety.

"You better remember that if you dare hurt Caleb," he continued without missing a beat.

I didn't know if I should feel comforted that he was willing to stand up to protect me or worried that he'd just threatened to commit murder. Instead of going down that rabbit hole, I ruffled his hair and pushed him to the trunk. "Go bring the bags in."

Zack, the brave man, followed behind him. "I would never

want to hurt Caleb. If I do, you can release your killer robots on me." Zack, the foolish man, clearly thought Conner was joking. I was fairly certain he wasn't.

He tentatively held out his hand again. "Truce?"

Conner appraised him for a minute before extending his own hand. "Truce. For now."

Mom greeted us when we arrived in the kitchen with the bags. She lit up when she saw Zack and pulled him into a hug.

"Zack, it's so good to see you. I'm so glad you could make it." She pulled him to the living room and gestured for him to sit on the couch. "Can I get you anything to drink? I have some cut-up fruit too." She fluttered around, handing him a pillow and even a throw blanket so that he was comfortable.

"It's so nice to see you too, Mom," I said sarcastically. "It is I, your favorite son, who you have not seen for a week."

She shot me a glare, then went back to tending to Zack and asking about his week.

Conner came up behind me, a lazy smile spread on his face. "You were never her favorite son." I tried to give him a soft nudge, but he dodged my hand. He reached to his back pocket and pulled out a piece of paper and handed it to me.

"What's this?" It was a rectangular paper that was folded in half. Opening it revealed a check for ten grand.

"This..." My head shot up, eyes wide with disbelief. Our family wasn't exactly considered poor, but we definitely didn't have this kind of money. "What is this?"

"I told you the competition went well. A representative from a large medical device company took interest in my robot and bought the rights from me." I looked at the business name at the top left of the check. It was from a fairly well-known company in Corio City, so I knew he wasn't being scammed. I stared at him in shock. I knew Conner was a genius, but I didn't expect something like this to happen.

"Wow...That's amazing. I'm so proud of you, kid." I handed the check back to him, but he shook his head.

"It's for you." I tilted my head in confusion. "Funds for your bakery. Besides, I wouldn't have had a chance to showcase my robot if not for you."

"Mom helped as well. You should give it to her." I pushed the check back toward him, but he refused to take it back.

"Honey, just take it." Mom came up from behind Conner and pushed the check back to me.

"But—"

"No buts," Mom cut me off. "You've done so much for us, and we want to do something for you. You'll need money for the new bakery, and this will help."

How did I get so lucky to have a family like them? I'd felt a deep ache when my dad died, but I never felt alone or like I was missing out on something. Because I had them. Their love and support slowly healed the hole that Dad had left behind and made me into a stronger person who was able to protect them in turn.

Tears welled up in my eyes, and I lowered my head, not wanting them to see me cry like a baby. I saw Conner's feet come into view and felt his arms wrap around me. Mom's feet joined him soon after, and she wrapped the both of us in her arms. A large, warm, and familiar hand landed on my other shoulder. I knew it was Zack's way of offering me support while letting me have this moment with my family.

"This means I get unlimited free sweets in the future, right?" Conner's voice broke the silence and brought a snort out of me. Mom and Zack chuckled. God, I loved these people. And the more I spent time with him, the more I realized my love extended to Zack as well.

Zack lay on the couch as I finished drying the dishes from dinner later that night. I sang the song that had been stuck in my head all day, and Zack occasionally joined in when I got to a part he knew. When I was done, I dried my hands and took the seat beside him. I grabbed his arm and slung it around my shoulders as I snuggled into him.

"So..." I started. "I was thinking about the bakery."

"What about it?" Zack turned his head and placed a gentle kiss in my hair.

I fiddled with my fingers, nerves shot at the question I was about to ask. "I know you said you wanted to leave your job and maybe start your own small consulting business here in the city. I was thinking that maybe it would be nice if I could hire you. Your services, I mean, for the bakery. Of course, I wouldn't be able to afford much since I'm about to get myself into massive debt, but I could offer something."

Zack pushed me down on the couch and straddled me, his signature smirk pasted on his face. "Oh, I'm sure we could work something out." He leaned down and attacked my mouth. I wrapped my arms around him and pulled him until he was lying flush on top of me. I ground my cock up against him, wanting that little bit more friction and needing him closer.

He pulled off me with a gasp, his breathing heavy and his eyes heavy-lidded with desire. "Bedroom. Now." His words came out as a low growl. I scrambled to get out from under him and to our bedroom. I didn't officially live here, but this place felt more like home than my own apartment did. And the fact that I hadn't slept anywhere but Zack's bed in weeks made it feel like it belonged to the both of us.

Zack followed me off the couch and crushed my lips with another brutal kiss. His hands roamed down my body and under my cotton shirt. My breathing hitched when his fingers tweaked my nipples.

"I love how sensitive you are." His lips nibbled the sensitive area of my ear. He said he loved fucking me from behind because he had full access to all my sensitive spots. I was quite sure that what he wanted access to was my ass, and god, did he love playing with it. My ass clenched from the memory of the nights he'd teased my ass cheeks with his bites and squeezes until they were completely red and tender to the touch. It was like he was training that specific erogenous zone to crave his touch. And it worked. The last time we had sex, he'd played with my ass until I had almost come from just his teasing.

A mewl escaped my mouth, and my cock throbbed, begging for release from its constraints. I took a step back and flung my shirt over my head. Zack looked down at my flushed body, almost drooling. I chuckled and reached down for the zipper of his pants. "Hurry up," I whispered as I kissed the sensitive spot on his nape. He wasn't the only one who had been exploring.

Another growl rumbled in his chest as he ripped his shirt off and pulled me close again. His mouth captured mine in another kiss, and his hands fumbled with the buttons on my pants. He had my zipper down when his phone rang with a notification. His hand froze as he glanced at the phone he'd left on the couch.

"Zack, look at it later. Please, baby?" I continued pressing kisses along his collarbone and back up his neck.

"Sweets, you know one of my clients has their grand opening tonight. Even though I didn't have to attend, I still need to be on call if they need me."

I groaned in frustration because I knew he was right. He never did things halfheartedly, and that was one of the things I loved about him. "Fine," I huffed as I released him. He sank onto the couch as he grabbed his phone. "But I'm not stopping." I crawled on his lap and ground my cock against his and went back to attacking his sensitive nape. I was getting off tonight even if it meant having to dry-hump him to do it.

"Ngh, babe, I...I won't be able to focus if you keep doing that." Zack's breath hitched, but he didn't push me away.

"That's the point." I pressed open-mouthed kisses on his bare chest. Moving down his chest, I sucked his hard nipples. Zack let out a hiss. I turned my head and saw him frantically swiping on his phone to open the notification he received. When he opened the new email, his body froze beneath mine.

"Huh." Zack sounded mildly confused, and his expression sobered.

"What's wrong?" I reluctantly removed my mouth from his body and turned to take a closer look at the email.

"I...I got a job offer. From Muse Hospitality."

I furrowed my brows. Zack once off-handedly mentioned that he'd dreamed of working at Muse Hospitality when he was in college. "I didn't know you applied for them. They're hiring in Corio City?"

"Yeah, um, I applied a while back and forgot about it. They never reached out to me for an interview, so I figured I didn't get the job. The email said they've heard of my achievements and heard outstanding praise from restaurants I've worked with in the past, so they want to hire me. And um, the job is on the other coast..."

It was my turn to freeze. The other coast...That meant leaving Corio City. Leaving me. "Are...Are you gonna take it?" I didn't look at him. I couldn't.

"I..." he started, but I covered his mouth, regretting asking him the question in the first place. I didn't want to hear him say it out loud because I already knew the answer. Of course he was going to accept it. Sure, he talked about opening his own business, but this was the company he'd dreamed of since college. I wasn't part of the hospitality industry, but even I'd heard of Muse Hospitality's prestige. They were the elites. The place people in the industry fought to join to advance their career. People didn't turn down job offers from them.

"I don't want to talk anymore. Tell me tomorrow." I lunged at him, not giving him a chance to speak as I attacked his mouth with renewed effort. If Zack was leaving me, then I wanted to have tonight at least. I'd be selfish tonight and drown myself in pleasure until I forgot about the deep ache that gutted my stomach at the thought of him not being by my side.

Tomorrow, I'd be the understanding boyfriend who supported his partner in his dreams. Tomorrow, I'd tell him we'd be the one couple who beat the statistics and actually made long distance work. That could all wait for tomorrow. But for now I could still pretend for one more night, in this bubble, before everything changed and reality came crashing down on me.

Zack was stiff at first, but he didn't fight me. He gripped my butt and stood up while carrying me. I loved it when he did that. There was nothing sexier than when your man showed off his muscle strength. Zack slowly carried me to our bedroom while I sucked on his tongue like it was the most delicious dessert in the world.

Moments later, he dropped me on our soft bed. He crawled above me to turn on our bedside lamps. He liked to see me when we made love. I was shy at first, self-conscious about how the blush starkly contrasted to my pale skin, but all my worries disappeared when I saw the awe and love in Zack's eyes. His eyes told me I was beautiful, and his kisses showed me how much he loved seeing me flushed and writhing under him.

With Zack above me, I loosened his pants and released his throbbing cock. I grabbed his ass and pulled him down, feeding his cock into my mouth.

"Oh Lord. Your mouth is as sweet as you are." Zack bit out

the words. He threaded a hand through my hair and gently pushed my head closer to his groin. I wasn't at the point of deep-throating him yet, but it was fun to practice. I sucked him in deeper and was rewarded with a sexy moan.

"Sweets, this is gonna be over way too quickly if you keep doing that. I wanna touch you." He pulled himself off me and replaced his cock with his tongue, groaning when he tasted himself. His hands slid down in a frantic need to get my pants off as I did the same with his. Once we were both completely naked, I flipped us over until he lay on the mattress with me on top of him. My ass lined up with his dick, and I ground down. Another moan slipped from his lips, and his fingers kneaded my ass cheeks.

"Give me the lube." His hand reached inside the bedside table drawer and patted around until he found what he was looking for. He handed over the lube, then ripped the condom package and suited himself up. I made quick work of lubing my fingers and loosening myself up for him. I was still sensitive from the night before when Zack spent hours opening me up with his tongue, his fingers, and then his dick, so it didn't take me long to prep myself tonight for him, thank god. I didn't have the patience tonight to take it slow. I needed him in me. I needed to be connected to him in the most primitive way and have the knowledge that he was still mine pounded into me.

My precum left a trail of white on his golden abs, and Zack swiped a finger through the mess and tasted it. "God, you're sweet everywhere." His hungry eyes set my skin on fire, and I ground myself against him, needing more friction, more contact, just more...

Zack must have felt the same. He was done waiting. He grabbed both my ass cheeks and spread me open, guiding me down onto his hard dick. We both let out soft sighs when he slid home. The hunger still burned in his eyes, but they softened and rounded with emotions that filled my own eyes with tears. I leaned down to kiss him and closed my eyes. It was too easy to fill my brain with thoughts of Zack leaving me behind, and I had to force myself to live in the moment instead of in my head.

"Claim me," I whispered against his lips. Zack's grip on my ass tightened as he pulled me off his cock, then slammed me back down. Tiny whimpers escaped my throat as he continued to ram himself up into me. His speed increased, and the pressure building inside threatened to overflow. I was so close to the edge, but I held myself back, wanting to come together with him.

"Zack...I'm close..." I warned. My nails dug into his chest as I took control of the movements, my hips grinding down on him at a frantic speed. I wanted to pleasure him. I wanted to see him explode, but I was so dangerously close to losing control of my own orgasm. Zack released his hold on my ass and covered my dick with his large, warm hand.

"Come for me, sweets." And I did. His thumb grazed over the tip of my cock, and the slight sting of his fingernail gently scratching me tipped me over. I came apart in his hand as he whispered words of praise to me. Spurts of cum shot all over his abs, and in my daze, I used my hand to smear it into him, wishing his skin could absorb it so that I could become a part of him. Zack's eyes darkened at my actions, and seconds later, he was also shouting out his orgasm.

"God, that's sexy. You trying to claim me too?" His face was blissed out. A wolfish grin spread over his lips. I was too drained to talk and could only grunt in response before collapsing on the bed next to him.

"Sleepy," I muttered, my eyes refusing to stay open. The explosive orgasm and stress from before took too much out of me. The only thing lingering on my mind like a ghost was the thought of not having this anymore. I claimed him with my cum and my ass. He was mine, and I was his.

He'd ruined me. I couldn't live without Zack in my life anymore, and I'd do anything to keep him in it. Even if it meant only being able to see him through video calls.

We'd make long distance work.

TWENTY

ZACK

Before I had the condom off and tied, Caleb was already asleep, mumbling about making long distance work. He had a strange look on his face earlier when I'd received the unexpected email from Muse Hospitality. I wanted to tell him how I felt, but he'd stopped me with his hands, and the broken look in his eyes made me hesitate to push. He truly thought that me leaving him was a possibility.

I was flattered to receive the job offer, and if I were the same man from a year ago, I would have accepted it in a heartbeat. However, things were different now. I'd have to leave Lady with Eric. I wouldn't have time to take care of her with all the traveling required for the position. The thought of leaving Lady behind, especially when we'd had a scare recently, was unbearable. And the idea of having to leave Caleb's side was...unimaginable.

There was no way I was accepting the offer. I wanted to tell Caleb and soothe his worries, but I got the distinct feeling he wouldn't believe my words. Instead, I'd show him through my actions just how much he meant to me. The feelings that had been developing from the moment I'd met him slowly filled my empty hopes until I overflowed with desire for things that I thought were impossible. I'd been okay without family. I'd been fine filling my life with a job I enjoyed and good friends. At least I thought I had been.

I should have known this shy, blushing man would snatch my heart. I'd always had a thing for sweet men. When he had first welcomed me into the building with cookies, and I had told him I liked sweets, I didn't know I had been speaking about him the whole time. He was as sweet as the desserts he made, but he was a sweet meant only for me.

Caleb's eyebrows furrowed, and he muttered something in his sleep. He didn't usually sleep-talk, so I could only assume that his worries had followed him into his dreams.

I needed to clean up after the claim Caleb had left all over my abs, and the lube leaking out of Caleb's ass couldn't have felt pleasant either. After quickly cleaning us up with a warm, wet washcloth, I rolled Caleb under the covers and turned off the lights in our bedroom. Padding into the living room, I grabbed the phone I'd dropped on the couch and checked my messages. My client had sent a message letting me know the grand opening was a success. I sent them a quick congratulatory reply, then opened the email from earlier.

It was strange how much one's perspective could change in such a short span of time. If I had received this offer a month ago, I might have stopped and considered it. But now, I had no doubts in my mind. I knew what I wanted. And it wasn't some fancy job on the other side of the country. My career was important, but it wasn't my main focus anymore.

Hitting reply to the email, I expressed my gratitude at being offered the position, but turned it down. A load I didn't realize I'd been carrying lifted from my shoulders, and I breathed a sigh of relief.

When I returned to our room, Caleb was fumbling around in bed, his hands patting the area beside him like he was searching for something. I chuckled and slid beside him. He immediately snuggled closer to me and settled down, falling back into a deep sleep. I gave his forehead a kiss and drew him closer to me as I closed my eyes. There was no question about it. I was home. To stay. And I knew exactly what I needed to do to show Caleb that I meant it.

I woke up alone the next morning. Caleb's side had long cooled, and the scent of bacon lingered in the air. Caleb rarely cooked, which was probably for the best. When he did cook, it was usually when he needed to do something to distract himself from his thoughts.

After washing up, I entered the kitchen and found Caleb closely watching the bacon fry in the pan. If he wasn't focused on the bacon as intently as he was, they'd probably burn. I walked up behind him and slipped my arm around his stomach as I pressed a kiss to his temple. "Morning, sweets."

He nuzzled his head into my kiss in greeting, eyes still focused on the bacon. I chuckled at how adorable he looked and snatched the spatula from his hands. "Why don't you set the table? I'll finish here."

He shot me a grateful smile before turning to grab our drinks and utensils. Caleb loved mornings. He was often up just as the first rays of light shone through our windows. However, he was somber this morning, quiet and reserved throughout breakfast. The few times I tried to make conversation, he would mumble his replies with a far-off look in his eyes.

I could tell he was thinking about the job offer. It was evident from the words he'd muttered in his sleep last night that he was convinced I would accept the job and leave him. I knew anything I said now would be wind in the air. I'd let him process, and we could talk later tonight.

While Caleb got ready for work, I sat on the couch and sent a text to Ian, explaining my plan and asking for his help. He quickly replied with a thumbs up, expressing his approval for the plan. With that out of the way, I sent an email to Joshua letting him know I was taking a personal day.

Caleb came out of our bedroom, confused that I wasn't getting ready. "You're not dressed for work. Are you taking the day off? Are you okay? Let me check if you have a fever." His confusion slowly morphed to worry, and he rushed to my side to place a hand on my forehead.

I removed his hand from my head and kissed it. "I'm fine. I don't have to go in 'til later," I lied. If I told him I was taking the day off, he would ask why, and I wanted to surprise him.

His shoulders relaxed. "I'm glad you're okay," he said, shuffling on his feet. "Maybe we can talk tonight?"

I nodded and stood up as well. "Tonight," I replied. I walked him to the door, and before letting him leave, I turned him to me and kissed him. It wasn't a hungry kiss like the ones we'd had last night, but slow and lingering. I wanted to convey all the love I felt for him. To make him realize that having him in my life was nonnegotiable.

When I pulled back, Caleb's eyes were full of longing, but also had a hint of pain in them. He opened his mouth to say something but changed his mind and closed it again. "Tonight," he said instead, turning to head toward the stairs.

When he was gone from view, I closed the door and headed back inside. There was a lot I needed to do before Caleb came back, and I wouldn't finish if I didn't hop to it. I sank back onto the couch and pulled out my phone to make some calls. Lady hopped up onto her spot next to me and kept me company. When I was done with the final call, I grabbed my keys and wallet and left for the boardwalk to make the final arrangements.

It was late afternoon when I got back to the apartment. Ian had texted me saying he was resting at home all day, so I popped over to his unit on the first floor to give him my spare key and the surprise I got for Caleb. The plan was that he would sneak into my apartment while I took Caleb out for dinner.

Thanking Ian one last time, I bounded up the stairs back home. I stopped outside my door and realized the truth of my words. This was home. I was never super attached to where I had lived in the past, which was probably a side effect of growing up in a house that didn't feel like a home. I always made sure that my place was homey enough to make me feel relaxed, but I never had qualms about packing up and moving. Now, I couldn't imagine living anywhere else but here. With Caleb by my side.

Caleb came home at five on the dot that day, weariness etched on his face. Now that he'd put in his two weeks at work, he was busy making the final arrangements to hand over his accounts. I got off the couch, where I had sat all afternoon anxiously waiting for Caleb, and followed Lady to the door to greet him. Lady rubbed against his legs as I leaned in for a kiss.

"Tough day at work?" I asked.

He nodded as he loosened his tie. "Had a lot on my mind." Knowing Caleb, he probably had a million different scenarios of the future playing out in his head. I grabbed his briefcase as he knelt down to untie his dress shoes.

"I thought we'd do something different for dinner tonight," I said, placing his briefcase in its spot by the door.

He glanced up from where he was kneeling. "Oh? What were you thinking?"

"It's a secret. You'll have to follow me and see."

"You're not planning on selling me to human traffickers or something, are you?" He smiled at his own joke. Once his shoes were off, I pulled him up and wrapped him in my arms. "Never. Afraid you're stuck with me," I teased, planting a kiss on his nose. "Now get changed and let's go."

I sent a text to Ian, letting him know we were leaving the apartment soon.

I drove us to the boardwalk area where we usually paused our morning jogs. People milled around the beach, and the outdoor cafés were packed with people enjoying their dinner. After we exited the car, we walked hand in hand toward one of the shops.

"Wait here," I told Caleb as I entered the busy café. I was friends with the owners of this place and had asked them for a favor. I had a picnic basket in one hand and a blanket in the other when I exited the shop.

Caleb's eyes widened when he saw me. "What's this?"

"Don't you think it's a lovely day for a picnic? Could you hold this?" I asked as I gave him the blanket. When he took it, I grabbed his free hand with mine and led him onto the sandy beach area. We found a spot a little farther away from the groups of people, a place that had a perfect view of the lighthouse and the ocean. I placed the basket down and spread the blanket on the sand. We sat side by side as I unpacked our dinner.

My friends at the café had packed sandwiches, crackers, and cheese, and an assortment of fruits. I smiled at the bottle of wine I found hidden underneath the food. They had also packed plastic cups for the wine. It wasn't the fanciest, but it would do. I handed Caleb a cup of wine and a plate.

Caleb looked over the setup and turned to me. "Zack, this is amazing. Thank you."

"Anything for you," I said, happy that the worry was gone from his face.

He filled his plate, and I followed suit. We ate while watching the waves crash in front of us, neither of us wanting to break the serene moment.

When the contents on our plates were devoured, Caleb turned to me and opened his mouth. He looked like he wanted to say something, but just stared at me with his mouth open instead. I picked up a strawberry and stuffed it inside his mouth. He bit down on instinct, and the red juice dribbled down his lips. I swiped his chin and brought the remnants to my mouth. I gave him a wink as I sucked on my thumb, just like I did all those weeks ago. His face reddened to almost the exact shade of the red berry, showing that he wasn't quite immune yet to my flirting.

"Come here," I said as I pulled him to sit between my legs with his back leaning against my chest. He snuggled his head into the crook of my neck, sinking into me as he breathed out a sigh.

"Thank you for today. It's the perfect memory for when..." He didn't finish the sentence, but I knew what he meant. He was still under the impression that I was going to take the job offer.

"Let's enjoy our time for now. I have a surprise for you later," I whispered in his ear.

He tried to get up, but I pulled him tighter. He settled with turning his head to see mine and asked, "Another surprise? You already surprised me with the picnic. You're going to spoil me."

I laughed. "Nothing but the best for you, sweets."

We stayed like that and watched the sun make its slow descent down the horizon. When the world was splashed in tinges of pinks and oranges, we cleaned up our picnic and headed back to the café to drop off the basket and blanket.

Afterwards, I led him down to the cliff that housed the lighthouse.

"Where are we going?" Caleb asked, but still followed me without any resistance.

"The lighthouse." I didn't hide it from him this time. When we reached the base of the building, I pulled a key from my pocket. Caleb gave me a curious glance.

"I called in a favor," I said as I unlocked the door. I lucked out to find that my friends at the café knew the lighthouse keeper and were able to borrow the key for me.

It was dark inside the lighthouse, so I turned on the flashlight on my phone. The light illuminated narrow stone stairs that led up. We walked up in a single file and entered the balcony that wrapped around the lighthouse. The ocean stretched out in front of us, and we were greeted with a breathtaking view of the sunset.

Caleb stepped onto the small landing with me, his profile painted golden by the setting sun. He watched the sunset as I watched him. Eventually, he turned to look at me and nervously pushed his fringe behind his ear when he caught me staring.

"What?" he asked.

"Hi," I said, thinking back to his flushed face when he had used the same greeting weeks ago. Back when everything was still new, and I was just the new neighbor.

"Hi?" he replied, tilting his head, his eyes wide with wonder.

I chuckled and shook my head, unable to find the words that precisely described how I felt. "I want this," I settled for. I weaved our fingers together and held on tight. "I want this," I said again.

Caleb had a confused expression on his face, but I continued before he could speak.

"Your dad once told you that lighthouses guided lost souls home. For the longest time, that was what I was. A lost soul floating through life, not knowing where I belonged. But you changed that for me. The first time we sat on those benches on our jog, you showed me the power lighthouses could have, and I listened. I listened and let it guide me. And it led me home to you." Caleb's eyes shimmered with unshed tears, and he made tiny sniffling sounds. I brought his hand to my lips for a kiss. "I love you, my sweet Caleb. You are my home. I can't imagine being anywhere but by your side."

"Does that mean..." His eyes filled with hope.

I nodded. "I rejected the job offer."

"But...they're your dream company," he said softly.

"They *were* my dream company, but dreams change. When I dreamed of working for them, I had no concept of a home. I didn't have a place to miss or long for, but it's different now. I have no desire to be constantly on the road. I want to be home, with you and Lady."

Caleb lunged at me. I took a step back to stabilize us as he slammed his lips on mine. He tasted like strawberries.

"I love you too, Zack," he whispered against my lips. His forehead pressed against mine as we breathed in each other's air. The sunset cast us in its gentle glow. It was the color of warmth and family and...home.

When the sun fully set for the night, Caleb and I untangled ourselves and made our way back down the staircase. I relocked the door and pocketed the key to return to my friend later. For now, it was time to head home and show Caleb my last surprise.

Caleb was more animated on the drive home. He gushed

about the romantic picnic I had planned for him and the trip to the lighthouse. He said he'd never been in one before and expected them to contain more than just a flight of stairs. I told him other lighthouses had enough space for rooms, but ours happened to be a smaller one. He proceeded to regale me with random facts he had learned about lighthouses, and I spent the rest of the drive soaking up his excited ramblings.

When we got home, Lady was at the front door waiting to greet us as she always did. She weaved through our legs, purring her delight at seeing us again. The sound of metal clinked against the tiny silver bell she wore on her collar.

Next to her bell was a key on a lighthouse keychain. It was an exact replica of our lighthouse. I'd found it one day when I was browsing the tourist stores on the boardwalk and knew it would be the perfect present to ask Caleb to move in.

Caleb picked her up and examined the collar. "What's this?" he asked when he saw the lighthouse keychain.

"I think this is Lady's way of saying she doesn't want you to leave. You see, she misses you terribly when you're not here."

A smile quirked his lips. "I feel the same. I miss her when I'm not here either."

I wrapped him in my arms as he held Lady in his. "Does that mean you'll officially move in?"

"I wouldn't want to be anywhere else," he said as he leaned into my hug.

We were pushed forward from the door slamming open, and a pop sounded as confetti and streamers flew over our heads. Lady leaped out of Caleb's arms, startled by the sound, but twirled around to swat at the rainbow streamers that floated down.

"Surprise!" Ian and Jason yelled from the door. Will stood silently behind them. He also had a party popper in his hands.

"OMG, congrats, sweetcakes! I'm so excited for you!" Ian

rushed inside and pulled Caleb out of my arm and into his own.

"You guys...What...How did you..." Caleb looked a little frazzled by the sudden intrusion, but still returned Ian's hug.

"Zack asked for my help to put the keychain on the collar while you guys were out. Plus, we were listening outside the door." Ian turned and narrowed his eyes at me. "Really, Zack? You used Lady to ask him to move in?"

I shrugged sheepishly, and Caleb laughed and laughed until his cute snorts made their appearance. I pulled him into a hug again and looked around at our tiny group of friends, then at the sweet man in my arms. They'd showed up in my world just as unexpectedly as the confetti our friends had showered us with. And similarly, they were vibrant and wonderful and exactly what I needed in my life.

I was home.

EPILOGUE

IAN

August

I leaned against the wall with a drink in my hand. Throngs of people milled about in the crowded room either congratulating Caleb on his bakery or sampling the sweets he had prepared for the grand opening. Caleb stood in the middle of the excitement. His cheeks were rosy from all the attention he was receiving, but a huge smile lit up his face nevertheless.

He shook hands with the man in front of him before turning to Zack. Love shone in his eyes, and Zack returned Caleb's gaze with his own mushy one. They couldn't keep their eyes off each other, and anyone who saw them could easily tell they were in love. I was ecstatic that my best friend had found his person, and they were obviously made for each other. When they were in the room together, Zack's gaze never left Caleb for long, and Caleb naturally drifted to Zack's side.

Zack had quit his job earlier this month and planned to take on local clients while he helped Caleb with the bakery. They made the perfect team. With Zack's experience in this industry and Caleb's delicious desserts, there was no doubt that this bakery would be a hit.

Next to Caleb stood Maryann, who had her arms looped through an older gentleman's. She had introduced us earlier, calling him her "close companion." The man, Julius, was absolutely smitten with her. I could almost see the hearts in his eyes when he looked at her.

On the other side of them, Will and Jason huddled close together. Jason gobbled the contents on the plate Will was holding in one hand. His other hand held a glass of water he had most likely prepared in case Jason choked. Will said something to Jason—probably telling him to slow down—but Jason ignored him and continued stuffing the desserts into his mouth.

I shifted my gaze away before my eyes rotted from cavities. I was happy for them. I truly was. But I couldn't help the bitter feeling in the pit of my stomach at the thought of never finding my person. Sure, Will was still working on his relationship with Jason, but anyone could tell they belonged together. Jason would realize that fact soon enough.

I, on the other hand, would probably end up alone. Nobody wanted the real me. They were only interested in me until they got what they wanted. It was a truth that was proven time and time again. I just had to accept that.

"Hey, man. What are you doing here all by yourself? I didn't figure you to be a wallflower." Scott leaned on the wall beside me and took a swig of his bottle of water.

I shrugged and took a sip of my own drink. I'd met Scott at the bar one night with Zack, and we'd hung out a few times since, but we weren't close. I couldn't tell him that sometimes I was so overwhelmed that I needed to get away, or I'd drown in the ocean of expectations that the world had placed on me, and the ones I'd placed upon myself.

"What about you? You don't want to try the desserts Caleb made for today?" I asked instead.

It was his turn to shrug. "I'm trying to cut back," he said as he patted his gut. I could tell Scott was self-conscious about his looks when I first met him. He hid behind loose clothes like so many of my clients did. But he didn't need to. He looked good, sexy. However, I knew what it was like to be filled with doubt, so I didn't comment.

"I heard you were a personal trainer," he continued. "I was wondering if I could book you for a few sessions."

"I am, and I can, if that's what you want." I didn't know if I should say more, but I did anyway. "Listen, you have nothing to be self-conscious about, but if you want to work out to be healthy, I'm totally onboard." I let my eyes slowly drift over his body. "Nope, you look great. Very *fine*." I winked.

He coughed. Thank god he wasn't drinking his water at that moment.

"I...Uh, I..."

I burst out laughing. His reaction was so unlike the rest, it was adorable. Most people flirted back, thinking me easy. They weren't wrong, but it was refreshing to flirt with someone who didn't look at me just for my body.

I patted his shoulder. "I'm sorry. I'm not laughing at you. You're adorably handsome, and I'm not just saying that to be nice. Have some confidence in yourself." I figured I shouldn't tease him too much, or else I'd shock all the words out of him. "Anyway, you have my phone number. Text me and we'll set something up."

Scott nodded. He considered it for a second, then shot me a smile. "Thanks, Ian. For agreeing and, you know, for the compliments."

"You're welcome." We fell into silence as we watched the people bustle around the room. Jason had dragged Will back to the dessert table and was loading up the plate with more sweets. Will was shaking his head, but he didn't stop Jason.

Eric wandered over to our wall moments later. "I guess this is where all the singles hang out, huh?"

"No, this is where all the hotties hang out," I said, and Eric gave a hearty laugh.

"That's true. We are hot, aren't we?" He nodded to Scott. Scott smiled and gave a small nod.

Eric turned to face the crowd and nodded toward the star of the night. "Can't believe Caleb gave him a chance after the ED incident."

"Oh? I've never heard of this. Do tell." Caleb had never told me anything about that.

Eric told us the story of the first time they met, his hands waving in the air in wild gestures. He had us cracking up in no time. I was laughing so hard, I had to wipe tears from my eyes. I looked over to Scott, and he was in no better state than I was. Our eyes met for a second, and something sizzled in the air before he looked away. I turned away as well, ignoring the spark of attraction that filled me. Sleeping around meant nothing to me, but I didn't sleep with friends.

I turned back to the center of the room and saw Caleb looking around. When he spotted me, he waved his arms and walked toward us.

"Hey, I was looking for you. Come on, we're about to cut the cake, and I can't do that without my bestie." He glanced at Scott and Eric beside me and flushed pink. "Uh, sorry. Of course I meant you guys as well. Please have some cake." He turned to look at Scott, his face reddening even more. "Zack said you were cutting down on processed sugar. I made dark chocolate-covered bananas and set some aside for you."

"Thanks," Scott said, shooting him a grateful look.

"Now, let's go. They're waiting for us." Caleb grabbed my

arm and pulled me to where the rest of our friends were waiting.

I might not have found my person, but that didn't mean I was lacking. I had an amazing group of friends who loved me and took care of me like I did them. It would be selfish to ask for more. I was happy. I was...

———

Don't worry! Ian will get his happy ending in the next book in the series: *The Flirty Neighbor*.

Want more of Zack and Caleb? I have a short story prequel that takes place five years before the start of this story. Find by subscribing to my *newsletter* or reading *here*.

LETTER FROM RYE

Thank you so much for giving my book a try. I hope you enjoyed the journey as much as I did. If you did, please consider leaving a review on Amazon. It really helps authors out. I can't wait to see you in the next book! <3

-Stay in touch by subscribing to my Newsletter! Or visit my website Ryecox.com

-Get teasers and early updates by joining my facebook group, Rye's Romantics.

ACKNOWLEDGMENTS

I am so thankful to my wonderful beta readers Conni, Sara, Lissa, and Kay. You all have made this book so much better.

ABOUT THE AUTHOR

Rye is an M/M Romance author who is a romantic at heart. She believes that love conquers all, and that's why her stories are guaranteed to always have an HEA. When she's not writing, she escapes to the world of books or daydreams about becoming a future cat lady.

SCAN ME

Made in the USA
Las Vegas, NV
16 June 2024

91127645R00132